French Roots

Adventures along the New Madrid Fault Line, 1811-1812

French Roots

Adventures along the New Madrid Fault Line, 1811-1812

Norris Norman

Parkhurst Brothers Publishers
MARION, MICHIGAN

www.parkhurstbrothers.com

Parkhurst Brothers books are distributed to the trade through the Chicago Distribution Center and may be ordered through Ingram Book Company, Baker & Taylor, Follett Library Resources, and other book industry wholesalers. To order from Chicago Distribution Center, phone 1-800-621-2736 or fax to 800-621-8476. Copies of this and other Parkhurst Brothers Inc., Publishers titles are available to organizations and corporations for purchase in quantity by contacting Special Sales Department at our home office location, listed on our website. Manuscript submission guidelines for this publishing company are available at our website.

Printed in the United States of America

First Edition, 2017

2017 2018 2019 2020 10 9 8 7 6 5 4 3 2 1
International Standard Book Number: 978-1-62491-113-2 Trade Paperback
International Standard Book Number: 978-1-62491-114-9 Ebook

Parkhurst Brothers Publishers believes that the free and open exchange of ideas is essential for the maintenance of our freedoms. We support the First Amendment of the United States Constitution and encourage all citizens to study all sides of public policy questions, making up their own minds. Closed minds cost a society dearly.

Project Direction by   Cheryl Lanney
Editing by   Janelle Reardon
Cover and interior design by   Linda D. Parkhurst, Ph.D.
Acquired for Parkhurst Brothers Inc., Publishers by: Ted Parkhurst

092017

Dedication

This historical novel is dedicated to Charles Allen, Sr., who was the author's Sunday School teacher, mentor, friend, and 'adoptive' father during the author's college years and following. Mr. Allen's exemplary life as a Christian, a businessman, and a family leader both challenged and encouraged the author to be all the more than just ordinary, but rather to live up to the purpose of God. He died in 1982 at the age of fifty-four from cancer. There has been a void in the author's life since. "Because he believed in me, I am all the more."

Norris Norman

Contents

Preface

Norris Norman has picked a very difficult subject for his book and has done wonders with it. There is probably no more obscure part of the history of Arkansas than the period in which this book is situated, namely, the second decade of the nineteenth century. Mr. Norman makes it come alive in a very convincing way. His main character, a French/Indian mixed-blood or *Metis*, is carefully crafted and is ideally positioned to tell the tale of the New Madrid earthquake, the early White settlers of a newly-American Arkansas, and the daily lives there of Indians and Europeans alike.

The author not only has a fine grasp of his subject and its sources but is also quite obviously a master wordsman. In my experience, this combination puts him in a unique position to describe the practical world in which his characters operate. The descriptions of the Arkansas wild, and of the only real settlement at the time in what would become the state, are bound to fascinate and instruct.

Norris Norman plainly loves his state and the people who have struggled here to make it what it is. This book is not just a labor of love, though it certainly is that. It is a revelation, and it will doubtless spur others to ponder and write about this most interesting time in Arkansas's history.

Morris S. Arnold
Little Rock

Foreword

THANK YOU FOR JOINING MY FRIEND, Jean-Pierre Villeneuve, on his adventure into the land of the Arkansas during the years 1811-1812. I hope you enjoy reading about him as much as I did creating him. My challenge was to develop a character who was both believable and interesting, and yet representative of the place and time. The story of his experiences must not only be a good read, but historically accurate.

Historical fiction is a careful blend of historical facts and an interesting story line. Of course, no one knows the exact details of history that occurred almost two hundred years ago. But historical fiction must hold true to history, historical detail providing both color and education. The history of a time and place must establish the parameters for the story line.

Much research went into this project, yet an apology is offered for any historical error the reader might find. A note to the author would be appreciated, complete with reference. Often, history did not happen as we have perceived it through television and movies. There is no acceptable standard other than exhaustive research. Unfortunately, there is not enough time in an entire life to know every detail of any age or major event.

In *French Roots*, I want to introduce the reader to not just the characters and story line which I have created, but more importantly to a time and place that I find fascinating. The middle Mississippi

Valley during the time period 1775 to 1840 was a dynamic theater of social, political, economic and cultural change. The resident Indian nations were being evacuated to the west by the American government. Also, European influence was shifting from French and Spanish to American.

Part of the book's purpose is to highlight the pervasive influence of the French in the middle Mississippi Valley. For that reason, I have chosen to develop a French character. And to add a French flavor to the story, certain place names, as well as the names of natural landforms, are written in French. I beg the reader's indulgence. All such references are explained in the footnotes. Also, a minimum of French dialogue is used to season the conversation. Hopefully, the meaning of this dialogue will be self-evident from the context. While such choices are the prerogative of the writer, my intent has been to honor the task of the reader. I hope that you, the reader, will be all the more drawn into the story by these cultural identifiers.

If you had lived in the greater Arkansas region during the time 1762 to 1840 and had been a traveling person, such as a keelboat man or a trader, many interesting characters could have been encountered. Daniel Boone was living out the remainder of his life along the Missouri River to the north. The destiny of the Louisiana region was being worked out among four nations to the south. To the east, Davy Crockett moved into western Tennessee and had already become something of a legend. Sam Houston left Tennessee to spend several years with the Cherokee in western Arkansas. The War of 1812 had emboldened the American nation. Mike Fink was plying the great rivers with his keelboat crew. Jesse Chisholm was building his Indian trade out of western Arkansas. Steven Austin attempted to gain possession of the land claim which became Little Rock. Jim and Rezin Bowie were becoming famous in south Arkansas and Louisiana. The steamboat began its colorful history turning the nation's inland waterways into highways for exploration, transporting goods, and spreading culture. Texas' war of independence was plotted out in Washington, Arkansas. The relocation of the Five Civilized Tribes was engineered and facilitated by the United States government. Though Charles Dickens did not visit Arkansas, he traveled through the Ohio River Valley during the 1830's. But the naturalist James Audubon did visit Arkansas during the time period. It was an important time in the southwestern expansion of the United States of America.

As one looks over a map of Arkansas, few Indian names are found. This stands in sharp contrast to Oklahoma. Most Indians native to Arkansas were relocated to Oklahoma by the government prior to significant white settlement. Place names in Arkansas are carry-overs from the settler's previous home or taken from the name of an early settler. Most of these are English, yet there are many French and German, and several from a wide variety of origins. The land forms were already named in French prior to White American settlement, such as the St. Francis River, Cache River, Illinois Bayou, Ouachita Mountains and River, and Grand Prairie to mention some of the better known. Some of these names were anglicized while others were left somewhat alone. It is evident from these names that the French had a lasting impact on the region we now call Arkansas.

The people of the time were a mixture of adventurers, risk takers all. Traders, trappers, hunters, and settlers risked their lives and fortunes in a wilderness land without roads, bridges, hospitals, or schools. The land was a wilderness by modern civilized standards. Woodlands stretched for a thousand miles, interrupted only by rivers and a few isolated prairies. Forests of hardwoods and softwoods, deciduous, and evergreens gave rise to sawmill towns such as Paragould, Arkansas, which produced trainloads of quality lumber to supply distant cities. The landforms included flat deltas, rolling hills, mountains, swamps, sloughs, great rivers, and fresh-running mountain streams. Animal life also was in great variety. Many species were pushed aside by man only to be brought back later. Besides the common land animals of today, elk, buffalo, bear, wild horses, wolves, and panthers were found by the first Americans to settle the area. As for the fish, catfish, bass, and sunfish were probably most numerous. But there were also alligator gar and sturgeon, prehistoric species still found in Arkansas waters. Animal products such as furs, hides, tallow, oil, and meat accounted for the early industry in the region.

The character of the land influenced development of the region. To you the reader, Jean-Pierre Villeneuve is obviously the main character of this narrative, but the land rises up in its own right. This majestic geologic area is a primary part of our story. I will look forward to seeing you again, *mon ami*, along with Jean-Pierre Villeneuve, in the "land of the Arkansas."

Norris Norman
Paragould, Arkansas

Chapter One

Fall, 1811

Perched high in a Chickasaw plum tree, a mockingbird sang a sweet melody from its romantic repertoire. On the ground beneath the tree, a rabbit munched soft grasses that grew along the gently flowing bayou. From deep in the woods came the bark of a squirrel. A light breeze blew through the trees, occasionally pulling one of the dry leaves from a limb. Overhead, a brace of green-wing teal worked their way south with the fast and choppy wing beat common to ducks. The sun shone brightly, warming the earth on a fall afternoon.

In a small clearing just uphill from the mockingbird's perch lay the still form of a man. He was dressed in gray cloth breeches, moccasins, and a bright red woolen shirt. A red *tuque* hung loosely from his head which rested upon a Hudson's Bay blanket. Stretched across the ground, his frame appeared long and lanky. His skin was dark, more than a deep tan. His hands had the leathery appearance of much hard use. His face pointed up toward the warmth of the sun. The angular face with a sharply defined nose, deep set eyes, and pronounced cheekbones gave evidence of a French and Indian heritage.

The long frame was so still that an observer might mistake the form for a dead body, yet it was very much alive. One might also speculate that this man was so deep in sleep that he was totally separated from the sights and sounds around him. That also would be a mistake. He was very much connected with his surroundings through his subconscious. One of the greatest geologic disturbances of modern times in the Mississippi Valley occurred in northeast Arkansas and southeast Missouri. The tranquility of the scene tended to soothe the man into the sleep of peace, but his sub-conscious read the sounds, smells, movements, and temperature changes for any indication of danger. With the exception of his horse, which was picketed in the meadow, he was alone in the upper reaches of the *Riviere St. Francois.*[1]

On this warm fall afternoon, Jean-Pierre Villeneuve dreamed of his mother and the care she had given him as a young boy. In the dream, he was playing under a tree with many low limbs. He climbed in and out of them, hanging from them sometimes with his hands and other times with his lower legs hooked over a limb. His mother sat nearby. She smiled as she enjoyed watching him play, yet alert to supervising his activity to ensure he didn't climb too high for his few years. In her lap lay a small buckskin hunting shirt that she was making for him.

The affection between mother and son was apparent, each enjoying the time with the other. The boy experienced the freedom of play and yet knew the security of his mother's presence. But whenever he saw her attention fixed on the hunting shirt, the spirit of the boy compelled him to climb higher than he ever had before.

"*Mahlili Falaya,*" cried Yahoh Chad, with a voice mixed with

---

1   The St. Francis River (American spelling) takes its beginnings from the uplands of southeastern Missouri. It flows south, joining the Mississippi River at Helena, Arkansas.

anger and fear, "You're too high for a little one. Climb back down here before you fall." She almost always spoke to him in the language of her people, the Chickasaw.[2] He knew he was much too high for her to reach him, but he also knew that his father did not tolerate any resistance to his mother's direction. At once he descended through the maze of limbs to the ground. Here she called him to her for a tender embrace. She was stern with him at times for his own well-being but preferred a more tender touch. The boy had wanted to go even higher among the limbs but now forgot that in his mother's warm embrace and flashing smile. It was a good time in a young boy's life as he could experience adventure amid peace and security.

A sharp sound jerked Jean-Pierre from his dream. He instinctively rolled several feet from where he had been sleeping and rose slightly to peer through the tall sedge grass. He looked around but saw no immediate danger. His horse was standing at the edge of the meadow, looking intently up the bayou, though with little concern. There was no enemy in sight, no telltale cloud of gray smoke from a gunshot. Remaining alert, he thought back to the sound which had startled him from his dream. All he could recall was the loud report, sharp and quick. He asked himself what else could have made a sound like a gunshot. The answer came then and embarrassed him, in spite of his being alone. It had been the slap of a beaver's tail against the water's surface. Earlier, he had seen a beaver

2 The Chickasaw (their dialect more properly pronounces it chi-kah-shae) people at this time occupied parts of Tennessee, Mississippi, Georgia, Kentucky, and Alabama. They are related to the Choctaw who at the time lived to the south and east. They were allies of the British and long-term enemies of the French. The marriage of Jean-Pierre's parents would have been unlikely, but never impossible when love happens. Mahlili Falaya in Chickasaw translates to Long Runner while Yahoh Chad translates to Tall Woman.

dam just upstream from where he had chosen to take a mid-day rest.

Fully awake now and disappointed over having his dream interrupted, Jean-Pierre rose to full height and stretched himself. His horse looked over at him as if questioning whether their rest was over. In response, Jean-Pierre spoke softly, "Can't stay here all day, mon ami, I want to reach the Riviere St. Francois before making our night camp."

Jean-Pierre needed only a few moments to replace the pack saddle and supplies before leading the long-legged horse in a westerly direction. The rolling countryside they traveled was covered in a variety of hardwoods. Occasionally he saw small game on the ground or up in the higher limbs of the trees. This did not slow his progress, since he was intent upon locating the *Riviere St. Francois* before nightfall. After their rest, he and the horse stepped along briskly. This horse was a recent acquisition from a trade with a farmer at Ste. Genevieve.[3] The man had complained that the animal was too fast a walker for common farm work. Since Jean-Pierre's fast walking pace had worn down several pack horses in the past, this one seemed well-suited for him.

So far he was pleased with the horse's ability to match him step for step, even throughout a long day's journey. There had been several of those since they had left Ste. Genevieve. After many long days now, they should soon come to the upper St. Francis. It was Jean-Pierre's intent to trap his way down the small river throughout the winter. Thinking ahead, he knew that the region was largely uninhabited, though he expected to encounter Cherokee along the

---

3 Ste. Genevieve, Missouri, was founded about 1750 by the French, and had a thriving French culture until the American migration overwhelmed it after the War of 1812.

southern part of the river.[4] He knew they had been displaced from their homeland in the east by American settlement. Now they were farming upstream from the St. Francois; juncture with the Fleuve Mississippi.[5] He did not anticipate any problems with the Cherokees. Once reaching the Fleuve Mississippi in late winter, he would return north up the great river to Ste. Genevieve. He hoped to trade his horse to the Cherokee for a pirogue,[6] which would be quicker conveyance upstream.

Without a need to focus on hunting as he traveled, his mind returned to the time when his parents were still alive. The memories of those years were pleasant. Unfortunately, those times had been cut short while Jean-Pierre was in his mid-teens. For many years, these memories had been acutely painful, but now he could remember the many good years which had preceded their deaths. Even so, the pain still lay deep within him. It would arise from time

---

4   After the Muscle Shoals Massacre in 1794 during which all the white men on a river boat were killed, some Chickamauga Cherokee relocated from the Tennessee River to the St. Francis River. In 1812, the Cherokee town on the St. Francis was the largest settlement in Arkansas, four times the population of Arkansas Post, the settlement of Whites. There were about two thousand Cherokee in the region. Though they trapped for the fur market, farming was the largest element in their economy. The next year they would move westward to the White and Arkansas rivers after the Great Comet. The show of such a great sign so close after the Great Earthquake the previous winter caused them to believe that harm would come to them if they remained on the St. Francis.

5   The French word fleuve refers to great rivers; only the Mississippi and the St. Lawrence in North America were so designated.

6   Pirogue is French for dugout canoe (pronounced pe-rohg). Whereas in the northern regions canoes of birch bark were constructed to furnish a lightweight craft easily carried around rough water, the Indian tribes of the southern woodlands traditionally hollowed out logs for water travel.

to time, surprising both himself and those around him. The memory of the time of his parents' deaths now became a distant vision. Jean-Pierre replayed the events as he had reconstructed them. His father, Jean-Baptiste, and his mother, Yahoh Chad, had been camped on the *Riviere Chariton*,[7] trading for furs with the local Sauk and Fox tribes just to the north of the river.[8] From the number of pelts found in the camp afterward, it was apparent that trading had gone well. Jean-Pierre had been traveling with some of his Fox friends farther to the north along the Riviere Des Moines[9] to trade with the tribes in that area for locally trapped furs.

It was Two Feathers, of the Sauk tribe, who had reached Jean-Pierre's party and brought him the news. He had stood numb as Two Feathers told him his parents were dead and described the camp scene as his people had found it a day after the fight. That scene and the speculation about exactly what had happened long ago had been burned into his mind.

In his mind's eye, he could now see the dozen Osage warriors make their deadly rush from the willows along the river bank.[10] His

---

7   The Chariton River flows from southeastern Iowa south through Missouri, emptying into the Missouri River.

8   The Sauk and Fox people occupied southeastern Iowa. Formerly they had been two tribes but had merged by the time of European expansion.

9   The Des Moines River flows out of southeastern Iowa and empties into the Mississippi River. The name came from the Moinagonan tribe, who lived in the area.

10   The Osage people occupied an area that included parts of Missouri, Arkansas, Oklahoma, and Kansas. "Osage" is the French representation of their name.

father had been skinning a deer, and his mother had been tending a pot over the cooking fire. Apparently, the fight had taken less than a moment to finish, but lives had been permanently altered during the brief encounter. Jean-Baptiste had shot one of the attacking Osage and then running to protect his wife had wielded the discharged firearm as a club, striking first one Osage, then another. When that weapon was torn from his grasp, he had taken out his tomahawk. While shielding his wife, he had sunk it into the skull of another attacker. Badly outnumbered, his father had been beaten to the ground with a war club. While clutching her fallen husband, Yahoh Chad had suffered the same fate. Jean-Pierre had found some comfort in their deaths coming quickly, with no opportunity for torture.

Even now these memories were painful. But by now the intensity of that pain had been dulled, being replaced most times with the many pleasant memories of their lives. On this day he was thinking of the time his father had taught him to build fish traps when the ground began to drop into a valley of large timber. Apparently, the rich alluvial soil in the valley floor and abundant supply of water made possible a heavier growth of timber than on the plateau behind them. Here grew walnuts and beeches, oaks, and hickories.

Sensing he was nearing his objective, Jean-Pierre looked about more intently as they turned westward to find the river channel. He did take the time to shoot two rabbits which bounded into his path. About one-half league farther, the channel of the *Riviere St. Francois* appeared before them.[11] It was a small river here near its

---

11 A *league* was a French unit of distance. There is much confusion

headwaters, and clear from its gravel and sand bottom. Trees grew thick along its banks. The horse was given time to drink from the river before moving on downstream.

Jean-Pierre's trained frontiersman's eye watched everything about them as they moved downstream. He studied the area for any sign of game, particularly those bearing furs. It was almost dark an hour later when he tied the horse to a small beech tree. His chosen stopping place was next to a small clearing where his horse could graze. Also, a fallen sycamore which had lain several years would supply dry wood for a cook fire. He unpacked the horse and hobbled it before turning it loose to graze on its own. By now it could be trusted to stay close by, especially if a camp was set up.

Jean-Pierre's camp contained only the bare necessities for a fur trapper. A sheet of canvas made up a half-faced shelter to give some protection from wind and rain. His few utensils would cook his limited fare and boil his coffee. The buckskin bags containing his foodstuffs were hung from a high overhanging limb to protect them from hungry animals while Jean-Pierre was away from the camp.

It didn't require much time or effort to make his camp. The last fading twilight found Jean-Pierre smoking his pipe in front of the fire while waiting for his coffee to boil. His meal was the two rabbits he had shot that afternoon. After dinner, he would set out some lines for fish. Hopefully, by morning he would have fresh fish to begin the day. As he sat alone before the fire, the flames lulled his mind back to memories of fires in other camps along other rivers. His mind went back to the winter he and his parents had been

about its length, but the most common usage is approximately three miles.

trapping in the hilly plateau south of *La Belle Riviere*. [12] Their camp-site, a location well-used for many years by countless other trappers and travelers, was near a bluff overlooking the *Riviere des Chauoua-nons*.[13] Jean-Pierre clearly remembered the beauty of the bluff along the river at nightfall, with a night camp set just away from the river's edge. There was a nearby spring for fresh water. This bluff had been their camp in years past, and that of many other French traders who had come before them. Because of its use by the French and because of a surface deposit of salt nearby which attracted local game, the location had been named French Lick.[14] Although the trapping had been good for a while, there were no local Indians with whom to trade. A curious thing had caught their attention. There was a field of corn in the area but no sign of any Indian camp nearby.

It had been their intent to stay several weeks in this area before pushing on upstream into the land of the Cherokee. But their trap-ping had met with interruptions. First, a hard freeze had sealed over not only the smaller creeks nearby, but the river as well. They had resigned to wait it out as there was no way to relocate by pirogue.

---

12   The French called the Ohio River *"La Belle Riviere"* or "the beautiful river."

13   *"Riviere des Chauouanons"* is now named the Cumberland River. Its French name came from the Chauouanon Indians who lived near its mouth during the time of the early French explorers. The Cumberland name was applied about 1750 by Dr. Thomas Walker, a Virginia land speculator seeking a land grant of 800,000 acres in the area of "Kentakee" (Kentucky). It was named after the Duke of Cumberland, whom Dr. Walker had met in England some years previous.

14   The location of French Lick is the present site of Nashville, Tennessee, along the Cumberland River. The expedition of Americans mentioned was the Donelson party of 1780. Their families along with their household goods were at the same time floating down the Tennessee River to the Ohio, where they would then work their way up the Cumberland to reach French Lick.

Then, one day, a large group of Americans with horses and cattle arrived at the eastern bank and proceeded to cross the river on the ice. Jean-Baptiste had visited with them and learned that they were settlers from eastern Tennessee, planning to settle in this spot due to the high elevation and abundance of water.

They told Jean-Pierre that their families and household goods were soon to arrive, floating down the river the Americans were calling the Tennessee. Jean-Baptiste also learned that one of these Americans had planted the corn the previous spring when he had chosen this location for a settlement.

Jean-Pierre's family had known that an American named Daniel Boone had found a pass through the mountains from east Tennessee to open the valley drained by this river. American settlers were just now beginning to venture this far west. Here trails and rivers were still the only routes of travel. Jean-Pierre remembered that it was many years later before anything resembling a road was built as far west as that campsite along the bluff.

Jean-Baptiste had broken his camp as soon as the ice melted off the river sufficiently to allow travel. He wanted to get away from the disturbance the Americans had created in the local woods. Jean-Pierre's family had gone downriver to *LaBelle Riviere*. They would never return to this area, as the white man's settlements disturbed the game too much for good trapping. Also, the coming of the American settlers always displaced local Indian villages, which were the principal source of furs for the French.

Camped now among the tall timber along the *Riviere St. Francois*, Jean-Pierre was pleased to be away from settlements. The many years of traveling with Jean-Baptiste and Yahoh Chad had ingrained within him a desire to travel. Whether along the rivers and bayous by pirogue or the many trails by foot or horse, he treasured being alone in his camp. His personal needs were not great, and he felt no demand to seek wealth. He carried only a few possessions, leaving most of his belongings back in Ste. Genevieve with his longtime friend, Louis Charlivoix.

Looking away from his small fire out into the semi-darkness of the tree tops, he scanned the clear sky with its multitude of stars. He wondered if this place too would one day be occupied by a settlement. The thought displeased him as he loved the land as it was now, open to the French trader as well as the Indian. Being both, Jean-Pierre felt a strong kinship with the wild woodlands of the middle Mississippi Valley. He had explored most of what the French called the Illinois country, that country either side of the Mississippi and above *La Belle Riviere*. Like other Frenchmen, he had traveled mostly by pirogue, using the rivers and streams as trade routes. This was his first time to work southwest into what was being called the land of the Arkansas. He knew that several leagues to the west were mountains with swift flowing streams which beckoned to a Frenchman in a pirogue.[15]

After knocking out his pipe on one of the fire logs, Jean-Pierre rose and carried his fishing lines to the river bank. Here he attached each to an overhanging limb and tossed the baited hook into the river. He knew that such small rivers contained a variety of fish. He stood there as immobile as a tree, becoming one with the life of the river. For some time he stood gazing upon the shining surface of the slowly moving river, taking in every detail of current, snags,

---

15　The name of the Ozark Mountains appears to be a corruption of "aux Arkansas" (of the Arkansas). Early in the time of American settlement, "Arkansas" was often spelled with a "w" as the last character.

sandbars, and the tree-lined banks. The partial moon gave enough light for Jean-Pierre to clearly view the scene before him. His left cheek sensed a light breeze from downriver, and his right ear caught the sounds of fish feeding in upstream shallows.

Later, back at his camp, he rolled out his Hudson Bay blankets under the canvas and lay watching the fire burn itself down. Overhead the light night breeze caused the dry leaves to rattle lightly against one another. Again his mind returned to times past. He thought back over the changes which were sweeping the Mississippi Valley. He wondered how many more changes could occur as the region had already dramatically changed in his lifetime. The American colonists along the Atlantic had rebelled against England and gained their independence. That had affected the frontier in many ways. Jean-Pierre still had vivid memories of the English attack upon St. Louis.[16] He had only been eighteen years of age at the time but had stood alongside the Spanish with the other Frenchmen to defend their city.

He thought back over the past tensions between the Spanish and the Kentuckians who regularly used the great inland rivers to ship their goods to the port at Nouvelle Orleans. River shipment was much cheaper than the overland journey to the eastern seaboard cities.

Twice, Spain had blockaded the river to all Kentucky river traffic, causing much hardship in that quarter. No longer could Spain flex its muscle against the Americans as France had sold all of

---

16 In 1780 (during the American Revolution) the British army came down the Mississippi River and attacked St. Louis as part of their effort to gain possession of the interior of the continent. At the time Spain was in ownership (European) of the region.

La Louisiane to the new United States.

During the Spanish rule, French culture had continued as it had in the hundred years previous. The Spanish had built few settlements and had imposed no severe changes upon the French.[17] The Spanish had allowed the French to be themselves and the culture of the area had remained heavily French in architecture, language, and general lifestyle. This was due in part to Spain's only influence being a small military contingent with little or no Spanish citizenry. But now many Americans were moving west of the river, bringing much change with them in language and culture. The river towns like his Ste. Genevieve were being inundated by American settlers, causing a definite change in their culture. Now the Americans kept a small part of their army west of the Mississippi.

Jean-Pierre himself had never served in any army, though he had fought and on a few occasions had taken the lives of others in his own defense. French traders by nature usually got along well with the Indian tribes, as their activity brought much-needed articles of European manufacture such as axes, pots, fish hooks, and needles, as well as the trade guns.[18] As opposed to the Americans, the French were not in the habit of setting up new settlements which infringed upon Indian lands. On occasion, a French trader in isolated areas could find himself threatened by enemies, white or

---

17   The Louisiana Purchase occurred in 1803 when President Thomas Jefferson bought all the Louisiana region from the French (Napoleon) for $15,000,000. The Spanish were still governing certain posts when the Americans assumed control.

18   Special goods were manufactured specifically for trade on the western frontier. While of reasonable quality, these items often lacked the frills and fancy touches found on items manufactured for sale in Europe and the American east coast. The term "Trade Gun" is a reference to such a product.

red. The English were a constant threat, as were the Osage. Though most tribes could be very hospitable if approached in the friendly manner of the French, the Osage seemed to hate the world and fought almost everyone. Memories sometimes became very fresh when alone in front of a campfire. Sleep gradually came to the trapper there along the *Riviere St. Francois.*

For several days Jean-Pierre took furs from the waterways adjacent to his camp, finding the area profitable for his time. But as soon as the catch slackened, he traveled on downstream, not wanting to either strip an area of its fur-bearing animals or waste time in an area that was no longer highly productive. Also, Jean-Pierre was always drawn farther on, as he liked seeing what was around the next bend of the trail or river. Following this pattern, he slowly worked his way south down the *Riviere St. Francois,* knowing that at some point he would pass from what the French had called Upper *Louisane* to Lower *Louisane.*[19]

Much of the area between here and where the St. Francois joined the Mississippi, about forty leagues farther south, was named the Grand Marais by the French.[20] It was a low region of circuitous water courses and thick timber along with numerous large patches of cane and briars. Jean-Pierre held high hopes for taking many

---

19 When statehood was promised for Missouri, the Arkansas area became its own territory in 1819. This new territory included most of present-day Oklahoma. The French and later the Spanish had already given some recognition to the division between what would later by Missouri and Arkansas.

20 The Grand Marais meant "great swamp" in French. Marais is pronounced "ma-ray." The name was given to the swampy region in northeastern Arkansas along the St. Francis River. This region has been subjected to prior severe geological disturbances, resulting in a sinking of the land. The great earthquake of 1811-12 caused yet more sinking. Parts of this strip today are called the "sunken lands."

furs from this swampy region. He knew that it would make for slow traveling, but he was in no hurry. He had given all the coming winter before him to trapping the Grand Marais before returning to Ste. Genevieve in the spring.

He had just moved his camp farther downstream and had begun to set out traps when he saw the tracks of a small heard of elk. There was no question in his mind about the tracks. Though similar in shape to deer, their tracks were much larger. His interest was high, as elk meat was considered superior to deer. Also, the heavier elk hide made stronger leather. Two days later he finally saw them. The elk were feeding along the far side of the river where the timber sat some distance from the water's edge. This open area had grown up in grasses, providing good feed for the elk.

Quietly Jean-Pierre slipped his way through the cover of the heavy timber to the near bank of the river. Here he took careful aim with the fusil before firing.[21] After the roar of the discharge, all the herd but one young bull vaulted away into the surrounding timber. The bull had fallen instantly when the round ball had broken his neck. After wading the river, Jean-Pierre gutted out the animal, careful to keep the heart and liver, which he considered some of the tastiest parts of the animal. These two organs were rinsed thoroughly in the river before being wrapped in a piece of tanned deerskin. Normally, with a deer, Jean-Pierre would carry the entire carcass back to his camp in one trip. But because of the much larger size of the elk, he needed four trips.

Because all of this meat could not be used immediately, he dried it. Over a low fire, he hung thin slices of the meat on racks

---

21   21 A fusil was the French long firearm, typically a smoothbore. It was a well-built and practical firearm that fired shot as well as ball.

made of green willow limbs. The cool weather of the late fall kept the meat from spoiling before the fire and smoke dried it sufficiently to be bagged.[22] Jean-Pierre tanned the elk's hide by using its brain to treat it. All this work gave him something to occupy himself between the daily trips to check his traps.

After two weeks in what he came to think of as the Elk Camp, Jean-Pierre worked southward down the river. Always the river yielded raccoon, mink, opossum, otter, and beaver. Here he was alone most of the time. He had encountered a Delaware hunting party back before he reached the river, but here to the south, there was no evidence of anyone.[23] He speculated that the Grand Marais was not hospitable even to the Indians as it was thick with briars, cane, and sloughs. But this did not deter Jean-Pierre from entering.

Here the river slowly meandered around the cypress and cane as it made its way through the low bottomland. Many of the trees were massive. Trunks commonly exceeded four feet in diameter, and many of them exceeded six feet. With their lofty tops, they gave the appearance of piercing the sky. The rich alluvial solid and

abundance of water had given rise to a great woods.

The Grand Marais proved to be a difficult place to traverse during the winter. Due to the sloughs, fallen timber, canebrakes, and briars, travel was arduous and slow. Because the horse carried

---

22   Dried meat, as well as corn, was a staple to Indians and frontiersmen alike. It was ideal for travel as it was light and almost non-perishable.

23   Some Delaware and Shawnee people had relocated to southeastern Missouri in 1790, a result of European pressure in the lands to the east. The Spanish government encouraged them to settle in the region as a buffer between the hostile Osage to the west and the White settlements along the Mississippi River. When the Americans entered northeast Arkansas, there were no long-term resident Indian nations, but several small bands of eastern tribes moved west under the pressure of White settlers.

his packs, he was forced to wade every slough or backwater. And, with the dropping temperatures, the water became quite cold. Also, rain fell every few days. Jean-Pierre was wet more often than he was dry during this time. An early freeze brought him some relief as the muddy surface hardened, making for much easier walking.

Chapter Two

The Great Earthquake

Though Jean-Pierre never kept track of the calendar while away from the settlements, he knew that Christmas was only a few weeks away. Of course, he would not be anywhere near other Frenchmen when the holy day arrived. His plan was to continue slowly working southward through the Grand Marais until reaching the Mississippi sometime in late winter.

For now, he was camped beside what at one time had been the main river channel. He was in an area laced with sloughs and thick canebrakes on the higher ground between them. Jean-Pierre's experienced eye noticed many signs of furbearers, so he would probably remain here for several weeks. With that in mind, he chose a suitable site for a more elaborate camp that included a shelter. The shelter was made from a conical framework of light poles covered with large pieces of bark from a nearby fallen cypress. Inside, a fireplace was dug into the ground, giving some control over the fire. Here he could cook his meals and protect himself from the winter storms. The horse could find plenty of graze among the cane leaves while Jean-Pierre took advantage of the area's abundant fur-bearing animals.

Finding a hollow cypress a short distance from his camp, Jean-Pierre sawed out a square of the trunk wall which could be refitted as a door. Into the hollow, he placed all his extra foodstuffs and equipment. Here they would be safe from either prowling animals or people. With a dry shelter for himself and his supplies safely cached, Jean-Pierre enjoyed the favorable weather for several days. He worked his traps in comfort. His only other concern was gathering a steady supply of meat and fish for his own needs. This camp was the most picturesque so far this season. The woods along the Riviere St. Francois were beautiful, with majestic trees of many types throughout the bottoms. The fall foliage was brilliant with color. Hunting, fishing, and trapping were all at their peak. He often saw eagles glide from the sky to the river's surface to snatch a fish and wing their way back skyward. Jean-Pierre relished such experiences.

While he was at this peaceful camp in mid-December, an event occurred that would change the land and the people in it forever.[24] Jean-Pierre had been sleeping soundly for several hours

---

24   The Great Earthquake has been so named as it is believed by many geologists to have been the largest ecological disturbance in the greater Mississippi Valley during recorded history. The first of three occurred at approximately 2:00 A.M. on 16 December 1811. The epicenter was near present-day Marked Tree, Arkansas. Geologists have estimated its intensity to have been approximately 8.25 to 8.50 on the Richter Scale. It was felt as far as Boston and all along the lower eastern seaboard. There was a violent convulsing of the earth's crust, resulting in many permanent landform changes, one of the most notable being Reelfoot Lake in northwestern Tennessee. This lake was created by the quake, as the earth's surface dropped several feet. The land and timber near the Mississippi River suffered much damage along a 300-mile stretch. Acres of hardwood forests were thrown from the river's earthen banks into the river itself. Sunken logs on the river's bottom were loosened and pitched upward through the surface. All this timber-choked the channel to navigation until the current cleared itself. The water in the river channel was so convulsed that huge waves swept back and forth like a tidal wave. Many boats were crushed, others were left stranded on high land a great distance from the river after the waves subsided back into the main channel. Fortunately,

one night when he awoke to a strange restlessness. For several minutes he lay quietly, attempting to identify the cause of his disquietude. He thought he could hear a rumbling sound of some sort, but he could not identify it. Then he felt a slightest sensation of movement; not so much from outside the hut, but from underneath it. Suddenly, he found himself being tossed about inside his small shelter. Accompanying the shaking was a loud roaring noise. Within seconds the light framework collapsed around him. Jean-Pierre frantically flailed about trying to escape from the jumble of poles and bark. He could hear the piercing scream of his horse, apparently terrified by the earth's violent shaking.

After a time, the shaking and rolling of the earth caused the rubble of the shelter to slide over and away from him. Now free of what had just seconds before seemed like a trap, Jean-Pierre tried to stand. He felt a sense of desperation as the shaking and rolling of the earth was so violent that he was unable to gain his footing for even an instant. Once he was free, his chief concern was for his terrified horse. Only able to move by crawling on all fours, Jean-Pierre struggled to reach the frightened animal. By the dim light, Jean-Pierre could see the horse fall down, then jump up screaming in fear before falling again. Everything about them was shaking

---

few deaths were attributed to the quake. Aftershocks occurred daily until 1 March and almost daily for about one year. The first quake on 16 December was followed by two other quakes, one on 25 January 1812 and another on 7 February 1812. The epicenters for these quakes were increasingly northward. The last was considered equally as powerful as the first. In addition to the major quakes, it is estimated by the U.S. Geological Survey that 1800 small quakes or tremors occurred in the space of about four months. All quakes, aftershocks and other physical disturbances mentioned in this book are either validated by the U.S. Geological Survey or are documented by eyewitness accounts.

violently. A deerskin bag which he had tied to an overhanging limb was bouncing about like a child's toy. Trees were snapping apart and falling in all directions. Sounds of escaping gases could be heard above the continuing roar. And the air was heavy with the smell of sulfur.

As Jean-Pierre had feared, the animal's tether snapped. Realizing it was free, the horse raced away from the camp during a short lull in the rolling of the earth. It charged at full speed into the woods where it was quickly engulfed by darkness and terrifying noises.

Jean-Pierre was helpless. He could not get away, and there was no safe place available to him. Just in front of him the ground suddenly dropped, taking whole trees down with it. A large cypress just out from his camp lost its grip in the soil and fell across Jean-Pierre. Several of the smaller limbs whipped him fiercely as they slapped into the ground, but the larger body of the tree was held just above the ground level by stout limbs which pierced the dirt to either side of him. Below he could hear, then feel the ground being pulled apart. Frantic with fear, he cried, "Mon Dieu," and reached up to grab a limb and pull himself up to the trunk of the tree. When he climbed above the main trunk of the cypress, he wrapped both legs and both arms around it. Here he hung while hearing a sound below akin to a great suction. He felt hot air rise to his face and smelled the almost overwhelming odor of sulfur. Presently, he heard the sound of what he supposed was the ground slamming shut again. Jean-Pierre realized that had he waited on the surface an instant longer, he likely would have been buried alive somewhere deep below. Again and again, he cried, "Mon Dieu, Mon Dieu."

Suddenly, as quickly as it had started, the shaking and the roaring stopped, though the timber continued to sway back and forth for several minutes. Jean-Pierre clung tightly to the cypress trunk. He still feared for his life and was unwilling to trust the ground below. Throughout the remainder of the night, he clung there, occasionally falling into a fitful sleep despite the continued shaking. Not once did he risk getting down.

About daylight, Jean-Pierre was beginning to find the courage to step down when again the earth shook violently. Hanging as tightly as possible to the large tree, he watched the swamp's remaining timber shake like strands of tall grass on a windy day. This episode lasted only a few seconds and was not accompanied by the tearing of the earth or the escaping gases. Though relieved, Jean-Pierre remained in the safety of the cypress for another hour, all the while looking about in shocked amazement. If some of his possessions were not scattered about the area, he would find it hard to believe that just the day before this had been his efficiently organized campsite.

The frightened Frenchmen looked down upon the immediate area of the campsite but saw no remaining evidence of the hut or any of his possessions which had been inside it. Obviously, all of this had been swallowed up into the crevasse which had nearly claimed him. There were few articles still under the tree from which his food sack was hanging. At this point, Jean-Pierre was too overcome by the risk to his own life to feel the loss of his belongings. He was acutely aware that he was fortunate to be alive, and without more injuries than a few scratches.

As he surveyed the area, he saw several places where the earth had dropped sharply away. Most of the trees in the area of the camp were either fallen or broken up so badly that they were permanently damaged. Though there had been no rain, water was rapidly spreading from some source. Much of the high land in the area had settled and was already beginning to be covered in water.

After a time, Jean-Pierre finally found the courage to step down from the safety of the tree trunk that had protected him. After a few moments of enjoying the feel of the solid ground underneath his feet, he began looking for his horse. With nothing more than a short length of rope, he began working his way through the jumble of timber and earth in the direction the horse had taken.

The search was short. He found the animal scarcely a hundred yards from the camp, in a twisted heap with its neck turned in a sharply unnatural manner. From the patch of hair embedded in the bark of an adjacent scaly bark hickory, Jean-Pierre deduced that the frightened animal had run headlong into the tree. Due to the darkness of the night and the rolling of the earth, Jean-Pierre was not surprised. The horse's neck had probably been broken instantly, bringing a quick death with no pain. Jean-Pierre was glad of this, as he had become fond of his traveling companion. With a mixture of sadness over the horse's unfortunate death and regret over his loss of a reliable pack animal, he retraced his steps toward what remained of his camp.

As he surveyed the area, he saw a few of his camp items scattered about, including his axe. Gathering those few things, Jean-Pierre pondered his situation, knowing that all the equipment and supplies from his hut were gone. The greatest loss was his fusil. The loss of both his horse and firearm at the same time was going to have a serious impact during the coming winter. He knew he had to recover as much as possible from the cache he had made in the hollow tree. Jean-Pierre picked up the axe and began the search for the cache that held the supplies that could make it possible to survive this tragic situation.

Nothing in the area looked the same after the earthquake as it had before, so it took a while to find the place where the hollow cypress had once stood. It now lay like so many other trees, in a twisted and broken heap. And over it lay several other trees. Jean-Pierre knew that he was fortunate that his axe had been one of the few items spared at his camp. He now used it to cut away the debris covering the tree's hollow base. Relief flooded over him as he retrieved the extra equipment, foodstuffs, and furs he had entrusted to the cache. He found them dirty and wet, but mostly undamaged. All these were then carried back to his campsite, as its higher ground afforded some temporary protection from the rising waters.

Sensing that any animals not killed in the earthquake would flee the area, Jean-Pierre realized he should also leave. He spent most of the morning locating as many of his traps as he could find. Though he had experienced slight earthquakes before, he had never known anything of this magnitude. Separated here in the Grand Marais from all other people, he had no idea as to the effects elsewhere. He could not but wonder if there had been great loss of life in the French settlements along the Fleuve Mississippi.

As he searched the swamp for his traps, the scenery continued to astound him. In addition to the many trees broken or brought down, the ground had in many places separated from itself with one part dropping and the other rising. In some places, these drops were more than deep enough to hide a man on horseback. With everything in a jumble, it took some time for Jean-Pierre to find the river. And when he reached it, some thought was necessary to understand what had happened. The St. Francois was almost indistinguishable as it seemed that the river's bottom had been raised, spilling the channel water out over the now-sunken land. In places, the original channel had all but disappeared.[25] Sand seemed to be everywhere about the surface. In places, there were long strips of sand parallel to the river, and in other places, the sand was left in large circular piles. He determined that this sand had been forced up to the surface during the separations. As he slowly traced his trapline, he recovered most of his traps. He noticed the water level was rising to his knees in places that had been high and dry before the quake. He thought to himself that if this water did not recede at some point in the coming months, the highland timber like oak and hickory would later die from the inundation.

The rising water gave Jean-Pierre no choice but to move immediately to higher ground. After returning to his camp, he quickly sorted through his belongings. The lighter, smaller and more valuable items were then gathered into crude pack bags that he could carry himself, even though his progress would be very slow. Everything else, such as the bulky pack saddle, had to be left behind. He knew that he would have to count them as lost along with the items in the hut.

Jean-Pierre was driven by fear, both of the earthquake and of the Grand Marais. Both his French and his Indian ancestry had given him a terror of earthquakes. Knowing that he could easily have been swallowed by one of the many crevasses or crushed by

---

25   Indeed the St. Francis River's bottom did rise, causing the water to spill out, forming new channels. The land's surface along the St. Francis River from the Missouri Bootheel southward to Truman, Arkansas sank as a result of the earthquake. There is evidence that this area had experienced a major earthquake sometime prior to the one in 1811 and that the one previous had also caused the land to sink in the region. The fact that the French had already named the region the Great Swamp substantiates this assertion.

one of the many falling trees, he was visibly shaken. Believing that God had spared his life, he was very thankful. Now he desperately wanted to remove himself from the dangers of the devastation. He considered going east toward the Mississippi and a quicker route back to Ste. Genevieve. But he feared the Grand Marais far too much now to venture in that direction. As he was already west of the St. Francois, Jean-Pierre knew that the shortest route to higher ground was to head away from the river. Heading west in the opposite direction, he trudged through the flooded timber, ever careful of his step lest he fall into one of the many open crevasses hidden by the high water.

Though he walked steadily until nightfall, he was only able to cover about two leagues before giving up in exhaustion. His hurriedly thrown together pack rode poorly on his back. Besides being bulky, the pack was extremely heavy. The heavy and clumsy pack made it difficult to cross fallen trees or wade deep channels. During one such crossing, his right foot had slipped down into a hidden crevasse, causing his right knee to twist sharply. The pain slowed him all the more. All afternoon he had walked through cold water, sometimes almost up to his waist.

Finding a hummock[26] of high ground, Jean-Pierre dropped the heavy and awkward pack and collapsed beside it. He had known since the loss of his horse that his situation was dangerous. Over the past few hours the weight of his desperation had fully settled upon his consciousness. He reviewed his losses. With his pack animal dead, he would have to carry his remaining equipment, food, and

---

26 Such upraised areas yet exist in this region. They came to be called "donnicks," a Scottish word. Larger raised areas also exist, and were called "islands."

furs himself. The loss of his rifle and the problems that would cause were equally depressing. During his tiring journey through broken timber and high water, Jean-Pierre lost his focus upon his own life having been spared. Both tired and depressed, a heavy despondency settled upon him.

After some rest on the cold ground, Jean-Pierre slowly stood. A quick look about showed that he was on a raised area that seemed to have been uplifted several feet in the quake. The area appeared to be about one acre in size and looked like a good place to make camp for the night. It didn't take very long for him to gather enough wood for a fire. With flint and striker recovered from his cache, he struck a succession of sparks into the char cloth. The heat from the ignited char cloth set the dry tinder ablaze. He soon had a fire over which he could get warm and make coffee.

The ensuing warmth and the smell of the coffee brewing made Jean-Pierre realize he had not eaten all day. He sliced a portion from the only remaining meat in his food sack, a salt-cured buffalo tongue. The water had to be taken from the overflow, so he boiled it for several minutes to purify it before making his coffee. Sitting on the dry hummock before a heartening fire, with his cup of coffee and sliced tongue, the mellow and jovial mood typical of the French returned again to Jean-Pierre. He knew that somehow he would get out of the Grand Marais and return to Ste. Genevieve, though the journey might require several months. For now, he busied himself re-packing to make the task of carrying all his possessions somewhat easier.

In spite of the extreme exertion of the day, his sleep was fitful. It was late in the night before sound sleep came to him. This was brought to a rude halt, though, by a strong aftershock about an hour before light. It instantly shook him awake. With the violent shaking, the fear of the prior morning came alive. The shock was short-lived with little damage, but Jean-Pierre was unable to return to sleep. With the first light of day, he continued his exodus from the Grand Marais.

At midday, the continually rising ground, at last, brought Jean-Pierre out of the water. He entered the rising woodland with relief, but the heavy load and rising terrain were taxing. Even out of the water, his steps did not have their normal quick and long stride. It was a relief to get away from the wet lowlands where he and his bedraggled clothes had stayed soaked. At nightfall, he camped along a gravelly bayou carrying clear water.[27] This watercourse appeared to have originated in the high land to the west.

After dropping his pack in an area protected by some cedar trees, Jean-Pierre turned his attention to food. Among his possessions which had escaped the quake was a fish trap woven from bent willows. Light in weight, it had ridden out of the Grand Marais atop his pack. Now he placed it in one of the deeper pools of the shallow bayou with hopes of fresh fish for tomorrow's meals. His reserves of dried meat would not last long if he lived off them every day.

His sleep was fitful again that night. Again and again, throughout the night, he dreamed of the earthquake. There were rumbling and snapping and grating and sucking sounds as well as the hissing sound of escaping gases. During all of this, he feared for his life and kept reaching out for the safety of the cypress that

27   This water course is Locust Creek, which flows east from Crowley's Ridge toward the St. Francis River. It is just north of Oak Grove Heights, Arkansas.

had been his salvation in the Grand Marais. In the morning he found himself only partially rested and depended upon his coffee to stimulate him into activity. His mood brightened after finding two small perch in the trap. Removing these and resetting the trap in a different pool, Jean-Pierre returned to camp in a much better mood. With a fire growing in heat, he dressed the fish and set them over it using two green limbs. Now, with a meal cooking in front of him and a cup of coffee in his hand, his mood lightened and he felt much better about his situation.

Jean-Pierre began looking at his situation and the possibilities it offered. He knew he had to develop some sort of plan if he had any hope of eventually returning to Ste. Genevieve. He began to assess his remaining resources, besides his own good health. His hunting pouch had been lost, but his cache had held extra powder, lead, knives, flints, and striker. He now separated the items of the pack, laying them out on the ground for examination, cleaning, and reorganization. The lead was of limited value until he acquired another firearm and would be extra weight. However, it did give him something for trade should he encounter other trappers or Indians. The powder would be useful in starting fires during wet weather. The flint and striker, of course, were his implements of fire building. And, one of his two extra knives would now be his primary tool as well as weapon.

Fortunately for him, he had long ago adopted the habit of storing certain extra items of equipment with his food cache because living alone in the wilderness always held uncertainties. The cache also had held extra fish hooks and line, a small sharpening stone, and the head of a tomahawk.[28] But there was no extra rifle, or pack

---

28 Tomahawk is an Algonquin word for a small European battle axe.

horse, and he was walking away from the settlements where any such items could be procured.

Jean-Pierre knew that this rise in the land before him was likely the beginning of the high ridge which paralleled the Riviere St. Francois on its westward side.[29] His options were to walk southward along the ridge to the Mississippi, arriving just to the south of the fourth of the Chickasaw Bluffs,[30] or northward along the ridge until passing the lowlands of the Grand Marais. There he could safely turn northeast toward the Mississippi and Ste. Genevieve. This was certainly tempting, as after the quake he was anxious to ascertain the damage among the French settlements.

But the commitment he had made at the beginning of the journey to trap throughout the winter won out. It was not in Jean-Pierre's nature to turn away from something once he had put his mind to it. But going back into the Grand Marais and continuing his trapping there was not something that appealed to him. Still he

---

Commonly carried by Indian and frontiersman alike, it was more of a tool than a weapon.

29   This high ridge is named Crowley's Ridge after Benjamin Crowley who settled near Walcott, Arkansas, in Greene County in 1819. It stretches from southeastern Missouri to Helena, Arkansas, taking a somewhat crescent shape. The entire length is approximately 125 miles and it is probably no more than ten miles wide at its greatest width. It is theorized by some geographers that the Mississippi River, at a much earlier time, flowed west of the ridge, creating the wide deltas of the Black and White Rivers. When the Mississippi changed its course eastward to join the Ohio, it then created the delta between the ridge and the bluffs of western Tennessee.

30   Chickasaw Bluffs is a reference to the high earthen bluffs along the Mississippi River in southwestern Tennessee. They were named for the Chickasaw nation which resides to the east. There are four bluffs in all, numbered from north to south. The fourth bluff is the site of present day Memphis, Tennessee.

held a great fear about the place because of the quake. And, beyond his fears, there were two other good reasons not to return at this time. First, the small game would likely be scared so badly that they would have fled the swamp just as he. And, the fallen timber and dislocated water from the St. Francois would make for exceedingly difficult travel.

Now he considered continuing on westward over the ridge. He knew from other French traders that the ridge rose only a few hundred feet in elevation, posing little obstacle to his travel. He also knew that in the wide bottomland beyond there were several waterways which could afford him both routes of travel and opportunities of taking more furs. These rivers would take him southward to the Mississippi where he could turn back north for Ste. Genevieve. This decision was the one that drew him. He firmly decided that his course should then be westward over the ridge and then south to the Mississippi. To himself, he asserted that since God had spared his life amidst the great peril of the earthquake, then blessings of many furs and a safe journey would be his throughout the winter.

Chapter Three

Over the Ridge

JEAN-PIERRE DETERMINED TO REMAIN CAMPED along this gravelly bayou for several days as he needed rest and the trapping prospects looked favorable. He was still quite shaken by the earthquake, especially as a large aftershock occurred at noon. It was so violent that he, with his strained knee, was thrown to the ground. For some time he considered leaving immediately for the west but decided against it. He needed time to rest and rebuild his outfit, so he decided to risk the danger of future quakes.

Hindered by his injured knee, he slowly cut and gathered enough saplings to frame a shelter. The larger ends were sharpened and pushed into the soil to form a circle about eight feet in diameter. Then the tops were pulled together and lashed with strips of hickory bark. Long slender willow poles were gathered and tied around the sides. He considered himself fortunate to find cedar in the area from which he could break green boughs. These were interwoven into the framework to provide protection from the wind and rain which frequently came at this season. A smoke hole was left open in the top. His furs would afford him a warm and soft bed for his rest.

In addition to his fish trap, Jean-Pierre laid other traps with which he could feed himself in the absence of a fusil. Snares fashioned from strips of deerskin were set for the plentiful rabbits among the surrounding meadows. He considered roasted rabbit one of his favorite camp meats and usually depended upon the local rabbit population for many of his meals.

Having flushed a large covey of quail from along the bayou, he fashioned a bird trap from small limbs. These were lashed together to resemble a small hut about two feet square. The trap was simply placed in an area that showed evidence of quail feeding. It was set down on the ground, with a trench cut into the sod to provide an entrance under the trap. Jean-Pierre gathered some seeds from nearby bushes and sprinkled them into the trench as well as on the ground under the trap. He knew from past efforts that the quail, once finding the seed scattered in the trench, would follow it down and up into the trap. Because they would be focused on the light between the cracks, they would be unable to find their way back out. Walking away from the trap, he thought ahead to the clean white breast meat carried by the birds and wished for better cooking facilities to prepare them.

With a forked limb cut for a crutch, Jean-Pierre hobbled his way about the area. He proceeded to set out traps and gather materials necessary to continue his journey. His progress was slow, but again he was in no hurry. As he had expected, he caught several raccoon and mink during these days. With the meat from the raccoon carcasses and the occasional rabbits from his snares, he found himself eating well again. And, from day to day, he took a few quail for a delicacy.

In this manner he remained along the gravelly bayou for several days, allowing himself to rest and his knee to heal. It was a good camp with plenty of small game from the traps and firewood from several nearby fallen trees. His knee continued to heal and cause him less pain. To lift the burden of survival brought upon him by the loss of his horse and firearm, he began to construct certain pieces of equipment. First he made himself a combination walking staff and lance. Until his knee healed completely, Jean-Pierre would continue to need assistance walking, particularly on uneven terrain. And, he needed a more formidable weapon than just a knife. He selected a straight length of slender ash, cutting it to seven feet in length. With his knife, he trimmed it of bark and sized it until the large end was about one and a half inches in diameter. He chose one of his two knives for the spear point. The wooden handle was burned off in the cook fire so that the knife might be fitted into the shaft. By driving the edge of the knife into the large end of the shaft with a heavy piece of limb, Jean-Pierre was able to split it. Into this split, he secured the handle end of the knife blade to form the spear. This end was then tightly wrapped with strips of rawhide from an untanned deer skin.

At the lance's balance point, Jean-Pierre wrapped a woven pattern of thin rawhide strips to form a grip that would keep his hand from slipping. For decoration, he used some walnut hulls to dye the forward part of the spear a dark black. Then three narrow bands of dark red were applied by rubbing poke berries around the shaft below the grip. He now had both a defensive weapon and a spear for fish. Being alone in this wilderness with no horse or fusil, Jean-Pierre knew that danger might come from a hostile traveler, either white or red, or from a bear, wolf or panther. In the hands of such a woodsman as Jean-Pierre Villeneuve, the finished lance would be a formidable weapon.

Next, Jean-Pierre worked on some type of vehicle which would aid him in transporting his outfit overland to the next navigable waterway. To suit this purpose, he constructed a travois out of hickory saplings.[31] He knew that a travois would be slow and awkward around uneven terrain and logs, but thought the trade-off would be worth it. He could carry the weighty pack much more easily with a travois than solely upon his shoulders. Most of the weight could be shifted to the lower end to reduce the burden.

But Jean-Pierre spent most of his time in the making of a bow with which he might hunt game instead of waiting for it to be trapped. It was his hope to kill an occasional deer not only for the venison but also for the hides. Deer hides not only sold well but also had many uses around a camp. Green hickory was chosen for the bow due to its springy and tough nature. On such short notice and without proper seasoning of the wood, the bow would only be marginally effective. But with careful hunting, Jean-Pierre hoped to bring in some larger game.

For the arrows, Jean-Pierre chose small ash saplings. These were cut to length and scraped clean of bark. To straighten out any curves, the shaft was heated over the cook fire and then bent straight by hand and eye. From the carcass of a dead owl, feathers were taken for fletching to hold the arrow true in flight. These were attached with a glue mixture made from boiling down old bits of deer hide. Among the assorted small items in his packs, Jean-Pierre always kept a few iron arrowheads. These were of a variety of shapes, some being for deer, others for small game and even some for fish. They were attached to the points of the arrows by glue and rawhide.

---

31 A travois was a framework akin to a litter, though slightly triangular in shape. The narrow end was supported upon the shoulders of a horse, dog, or man. Typically it was made of light poles and overlaid with branches. It is a French word and is pronounced trav-wah.

Jean-Pierre now felt fortunate for having had an Indian mother, as he had been trained in such manufacture as he grew up. He had always used a bow for some of his hunting, particularly when there was need for silence. Now isolated in the wilderness without a rifle, such skills were invaluable.

After a week in camp along the bayou, he was driven to his shelter by a winter storm which sent a shower of sleet and freezing rain onto everything, making it both difficult and dangerous to move about, particularly with his bad knee. On his few forays to run his snares and traps, the beauty of the ice over the trees struck Jean-Pierre as being part of the wonder of God. Here in the wilderness, the freezing rain over the tree limbs had formed giant chandeliers of great beauty. He had seen a few paintings of such things, but never a real one. The thought came to him that the real ones in the palaces of Paris could not be more beautiful than the ones God had created for him here in the wilderness.

Jean-Pierre took the time during the ice storm to make some new garments to shield him from the elements of winter. These were necessities as the briars of the Grand Marais had torn his clothing almost beyond use. First, he cut and sewed the elk hide into a new pair of leggings and moccasins. Then, he took his poorest pelts and stitched them together into a cape to replace the capote which had been lost with the hut.[32] All this was slow work, but there was little for him to do until the icy covering melted off the ground. Also, he smoked meat over a small rack inside his hut. Fortunately, he had taken several fish, raccoon, and quail in the few days before the

---

32 "Capote" is a French word for coat. It is pronounced "ka-po." Frontiersmen commonly used the word to refer to a long garment made from woolen blanket material.

storm, giving him plenty to eat.

After three days, the ice had melted away with warming weather. Jean-Pierre then lifted the head of the travois onto his shoulders and stepped westward toward the distant ridge. He had no idea of the distance as he could not see very far due to the thick timber. Here, spread before him, was a wide, shallow valley drained by the bayou beside which he had been camped the previous week. Jean-Pierre assumed that the bayou's headwaters would be somewhere against the ridge to the west.

The use of the travois proved to be less of a burden than the pack had been. Slowly, he moved westward, dragging it behind him. Generally, he walked beside the bayou. He passed through stands of tall hickory, oak, ash, gum, and walnut, but occasionally there were meadows of sedge grass among the timber. He was tiring toward the end of the first day when he was surprised by half a dozen buffalo grazing their way south through the timber. Watching them from a distance, Jean-Pierre wished so very much for his fusil as a buffalo robe would surely help him sleep warm against the night cold. He thought of the bow tied onto the travois and wondered if it would be worth a try. He decided not to risk it as buffalo were heavily muscled animals. It required a bow of great power to send an arrow deep enough to make a kill. There was also the element of danger in that he was alone without even a horse to assist him.

After regretfully watching the last of the buffalo pass on, Jean-Pierre tiredly dragged the travois in search of the night's camp site. Too tired to go any farther and unable to find a natural shelter, he simply chose a dry area near a fallen sycamore. At least, he could have plenty of wood for his fire. With a little effort, a shelter was thrown up with his canvas to ward off the night breezes.

That evening he sat upon his furs before the fire with a cup of coffee and thought back to other days and other fires. Quickly, his mind flashed across different memories of his parents. His mind began to focus upon their deaths. Still there was the anger toward the Osage for what Jean-Pierre considered senseless murders. The attack upon his parent's camp had been simply an opportunity for the war party to inflict its hatred against anyone outside their own tribe. Very little had been taken from the camp, possibly as they were quickly retreating from their raids upon the Sauk and Fox villages to the north. Jean-Pierre reflected now that though few physical items had been taken from the camp, his loss in that tragic event was great, so much so that it could never be replaced.

Others might have taken the trail of vengeance, but that was not Jean-Pierre's way. He understood that the Osage were only acting out their violence toward others that had been so characteristic of this tribe in all the years he had ever heard mention of them. True, he had relished the opportunity some years later when he had accompanied some Delaware to regain horses and women stolen by the Osage. And, he had found himself pursuing the trail with a thirst, anxious to overtake the raiders. Later, Jean-Pierre had passed off his part in the battle just as he had the attack upon his parents, just a part of living on the frontier.[33] Those Osage that were killed had died the way they had lived; justice in the wilderness. It was still painful to Jean-Pierre that his parents had died so violently though they had never sought trouble with any tribe. Their only intent had been to trade and enjoy life.

The next morning found Jean-Pierre dragging the travois

---

33   The word frontier is French and means "front line, the farthest edge, or the limit of a region.

along with renewed vigor, even though the elevation was increasing and the washes and creeks were becoming more frequent. His progress was interrupted about mid-morning when a violent shock almost shook him to the ground. Only the travois kept him from falling as it balanced him. The trees nearby shook so hard that dry leaves not yet fallen rained down upon the ground and, those leaves already upon the ground shook like chaff. For a moment, he stood still to collect himself and guard against another tremor. With this experience past, Jean-Pierre pressed on, eager to move westward.

By noon, though, he was leaving the travois propped against a tree from time to time in order to rest. He took these times to search ahead through the woods for the easiest routes of travel. By mid-afternoon, the terrain was becoming sufficiently steep to cause him to rest frequently. Here the timber was smaller, probably because the soil would be poorer and the water less abundant. Thoughts of a campsite came to him as the sky was becoming increasingly dark and the temperature was rapidly dropping.

Nightfall found him camped against the base of a large fallen white oak. When the tree had fallen, it had pulled up and held a large amount of soil, making for a natural shelter from the wind. The tree itself offered a ready supply of dry firewood for his meal and to keep away the chill through the cold night. That evening dried meat made up his supper. Jean-Pierre reasoned that he was close to the top of the ridge, as the valleys were quite narrow here. He believed that one of these would surely lead him to the top of the main ridge by mid-morning. He had considered pushing on in the late afternoon to reach the ridge before his night camp, but had held back, as the ridge would be a very cold place to camp if there were no ready routes to descend the other side with the travois. Here he was sheltered quite well from the cold north wind.

He had been pressed to consider pushing on over the top by the vivid memories of the violent shocks over the past few days. In addition to the large shock early in the day, another had occurred just after noon. Jean-Pierre longed for the time when he had distanced himself far enough from the Gran Marais that he would no longer feel the earth tremble beneath him. The next morning held a surprise for Jean-Pierre as he woke and raised up on one elbow. A blanket of white covered everything. Two inches of wet snow had fallen sometime during the night. Though he found beauty in it, he knew that the snow would only make his uphill travel much more difficult. Relief came an hour later in the form of a warm rain which melted away the snow. The land's surface was still slippery, but not as much as before.

About mid-morning he crested the ridge just as he had expected. He could not see any distance beyond, but was sure that this elevation he had just attained was the main ridge line. Too tired to go any further right now, he propped up the travois to rest before searching for the easiest route down into the valley on the western side. For a time, he leaned against a large pine tree while catching his breath. Standing there on the ridge line dividing the vastness of the bottom land, Jean-Pierre considered that this was the highest elevation between the mountains to the west and the Fleuve Mississippi to the east. He now thought back to certain other travelers he had known. He remembered well when the American President Jefferson had sent Captains Lewis and Clark to explore the vast Louisiana Purchase.[34] Jean-Pierre had been in St.

---

34 The Lewis and Clark Expedition was ordered by President Jefferson after the Louisiana Purchase which reached from the Gulf of Mexico to

Louis recuperating from a leg wound at the time the young captains had passed through. They had stopped in St. Louis, taking time to gather last minute supplies and organize their party. Jean-Pierre himself had wanted so badly to accompany them.

Most of the French hated the British and only tolerated the Americans. Jean-Pierre, though, had enjoyed the company of many Americans in his travels and had seen instantly the wonderful opportunity this exploration party offered. But fate was against him as his leg was far from healed. He was fortunate in that he had almost lost the left leg to gangrene. He had been injured during a fierce attack against the Osage by the Sauk and Fox Confederation. Of course, he had been assisting his friends, the Fox. He had considered the serious injury a minor price to pay for the privilege of coming to the aid of friends and settling an old grievance at the same time. But when prevented from joining the American exploration venture, Jean-Pierre had many regrets as the opportunity to experience such an adventure would have brought him great pleasure.

As he stood now on the crest of this low ridge of hills, he again regretted that lost opportunity. It was two years later before the two young American captains brought their party back across the great plains. Jean-Pierre had been trading among his mother's people at Okahfalaya on the Tombigbee River[35] when the explorers returned

---

Canada, and, in the north, reached from the Great Lakes to the Rocky Mountains. This exploration party traveled up the Missouri River to its headwaters in the Rocky Mountains and on west to the Pacific Ocean. This was not the only such expedition, just the longest and best known. Another party went up the Red River from the Mississippi, and another west across Kansas into Colorado. A small party was detached from the latter to explore down the Arkansas River from what is now Great Bend, Kansas. All were military endeavors which sent lengthy reports back to the President.

35 "Okahfalaya" was the name of an actual Chickasaw village. A literal

through St. Louis. Some months later he had interviewed everyone he could find in St. Louis who had contact with the captains to learn himself of their discoveries. It had pained him to hear of the many experiences he would have had; the different Indian tribes, the great Rocky Mountains and all the rivers with different kinds of fish. But probably the greatest disappointment had been his not getting to see the great Pacific Ocean with water farther than the eye could possibly see across the horizon. Well, thought Jean-Pierre, fate had brought several disappointments during his years, but his life had not been so bad. God always seemed to preserve him and offer him another trail to enjoy. The Great Earthquake had almost swallowed him and had left him handicapped without a firearm or a horse, but he was alive, with plenty to eat and the horizon before him.

Now as he walked along this ridge, he looked out over the spreading valleys below him. They were mostly gray with the dormancy of winter, but large splashes of green could be seen in the pine trees commonly found here on the ridge. Several of the pines had fallen along the ridge, perhaps the result of strong winds sometime in the past. Since they were long dead, Jean-Pierre knew that it had not been the result of the earthquake. From these he gathered a great number of knots. These could easily be pulled from the decaying trunks, as the knots were full of pitch and decayed much later than the rest of the tree. Pine knots were useful in camp for fire-building and torches.

Finding a gently sloping point leading down into the western slope, Jean-Pierre shouldered his travois and slowly pulled it down

translation would be "Long Town." The village was thirteen miles long and seven miles wide and was located near present day Tupelo, Mississippi.

the incline without allowing its momentum to overtake him. It was tiring work, but the pines were particularly thick here and afforded him a rest for the travois upon occasion.

At the bottom he found a very small bayou and followed it downstream through a maze of small trees. At some distance the bayou suddenly increased in volume, causing Jean-Pierre to leave the travois against a small beech in order to investigate further. Shortly, he was able to detect a large spring sending forth a steady flow of water out of the base of the ridge. Here he filled his drinking gourd and took some dried meat out of his packs for a noon meal before pushing on down the small valley.[36]

After his sparse meal was finished, he gathered up his bag of victuals. It was then that he glanced down the bayou some distance below the spring. There in the soft damp soil were the footprints of a bear. The bank was so tracked up that even from a distance Jean-Pierre could recognize the tracks. On closer examination, Jean-Pierre determined that this was the regular watering place for a large bear. He speculated that the bear was denned near here and used this bayou to drink on the odd occasion that it left the den. Jean-Pierre's mind quickly sorted out the facts and the possibilities. A bear would be a welcome addition to his stores even though the meat might be tough by this time of the winter. Nothing short of a buffalo robe was as warm as a bear skin. In addition, the sharp claws from a large bear would make an admirable necklace to wear or to trade. Also, the fat could be useful about the camp. The fact that he had no fusil did not rule out the possibility of his killing the

---

36 This location exists as it is described and is known locally as Pine Hill, just east of Beech Grove, Arkansas. Arkansas Highway 34 comes down the hill and passes within a few feet of the spring.

bear. He knew that Indians throughout the region had always killed bears in their dens with nothing more than a lance or a bow. Of course, it took both skill and courage. In these moments Jean-Pierre examined himself for both. His woodland skills had provided him a well-crafted lance, suitable for the challenge before him. And, from a lifetime of woodland life, he knew that he had the nerve required to carry it out. After only a moment of thought, he stepped along what appeared to be the bear's trail to his den. As he walked, he thought about the risks of being alone in the wilderness. Any day might bring an accident, threatening weather or the attack of an animal. Other men, both Indian and European, always posed a possible threat. But, it was his way of life. Even without his fusil, he was willing to pursue this bear's trail.

The trail meandered through the timber and around a corner of the hill to wind its way up a narrow hollow. Within a few minutes, the den became obvious to the experienced hunter. A large beech was growing along the steep slope of the hill. Over the years, animals had dug an increasingly larger hole underneath this tree. Now it was bear that had enlarged it to shelter its body from the elements of winter.

After only a moment's hesitation, Jean-Pierre stepped along quietly in the wet leaves, easing himself forward with the lance point before him. Foremost in his mind was the fact that bears did not truly hibernate, but only slept soundly for long periods of time. He well knew that this bear would rouse himself from time to time and leave his den for water before returning for more sleep. The recent tracks verified that bit of knowledge. Now Jean-Pierre hoped that this morning was one of the periods of deep sleep, all the while thankful that the previous night's snow and rain had softened the leaves to allow a silent approach.

As quietly as possible, he stooped to his knees before the hole beneath the beech and cautiously peered into the darkness of the small earthen cave. As his eyes adjusted to the dark cave, he saw the bear lay just before him, seemingly sound asleep in a pile of leaves. Quickly, Jean-Pierre set his feet solidly on the sloping bank and raised the lance to align with the bear's heart. Thrusting forward with all his strength and weight, he pushed the spear's knife point through the bear's rib cage and into its heart. There was some movement, but shortly the animal again lay still.[37]

After dragging the heavy bear from its den, Jean-Pierre proceeded to dress out this animal to meet his needs. Bear meat was of poor quality in the winter as the fat was burned off to sustain the animal while sleeping. But as the winter was not half over, Jean-Pierre thought that the hams might still be tender. With much practiced strokes, this woodsman skinned the animal's hide away from its carcass, removed the claws from the feet, sliced off and collected the pockets of fat, opened the cavity and took its urine, cut off the hams as well as the front shoulders, and broke open the skull and removed the brain. When all this was packaged and carried back to the travois, he realized that the day was too far along to continue travel. Knowing that the area by the spring would make a good camp site, he set about getting a cook fire going to prepare his evening meal. Several large slices of the bear ham were set over the

---

37   Indians within the region sometimes killed bears in this manner. The hair was long and clean, good for robes. The claws had grown back out after a summer's digging, making them suitable for a necklace. In the Ozark Mountains where limestone caves were plentiful, bears were commonly found back inside the caves. It required a brave hunter with a steady hand to effect a kill.

fire to broil. He began wishing for some bread and vegetables, but knew that he was fortunate to have the bear steak.

Jean-Pierre felt good within himself as he set out the next morning through the timber. The earthquake had dealt him a heavy blow, but he was getting along well under the circumstances. Of course, his growing-up years had been spent in the woods, either under the tutelage of his parents or while visiting Okahfalaya along the Tombigbee River.

At first, travel that morning was slow due to the dense timber and twisting slopes, but the valley soon opened to broad flats with some open meadows of sedge grass. Here the going was much easier and Jean-Pierre pushed himself to get some distance behind him. The weather had quickly turned cold again, freezing the ground's surface hard like a rock. But the effort of dragging the travois kept him warm in spite of the cold.

He was surprised that afternoon when he came to the mouth of the valley so soon after crossing the ridge. Here he found a high, wooded table land stretching out before him. As he had seen signs of raccoons in the preceding hours, he determined to make a camp. He thought he would remain here and trap for a few days after crossing the ridge. His knee had not entirely healed, and some extended rest would assist that process.

After making his camp among a grove of large beech trees which grew along the bayou, Jean-Pierre worked his way up and down the small bayou setting out his traps for raccoon and mink, as the stream did not appear to hold any beaver.[38] In one of the large

---

38   This is the present location of Beech Grove, Arkansas, (Greene County) along the western side of Crowleys Ridge. The author's maternal ancestors settled there about 1844.

pools near his camp, he set out his fish trap as he did not know of the availability of fish or game in the miles ahead. Whatever fish were caught would be dried for later used as he still had more fresh bear meat that he could eat.

It was here in his camp among the giant beech trees that Jean-Pierre realized that in the excitement of the earthquake and his subsequent flight over the ridge, he had forgotten all about Christmas. After some calculations, he determined that it had to be close to Christmas Day, though probably not it exactly. Having no priest or sanctuary or even the company of other Frenchmen, he felt very alone. It was a cold night, with a clear sky full of bright stars. The brightness of one eastern star seemed to remind him that he was not absolved from his duty to worship God in this sacred season. Overcome by the thought, Jean-Pierre sought some special way to observe its holiness.

With no articles of worship to mark the observance, Jean-Pierre approached one of the giant beeches which stood within his firelight. Taking his knife, he began to carve an altar of sorts into the smooth leathery bark of the beech. First, he pulled the knife in two intersecting straight lines to remove strips of bark, leaving the bold image of a cross. The yellow underlayer shone brightly like gold. Below the cross he carved in four-inch letters A M D G.[39] Then using letters about half as large as before, he carved his own name, Jean-Pierre Villeneuve, and the date 25 Decembre 1811. Finished with the altar, Jean-Pierre reached back to his cook fire and lit three of the pine knots. With these burning brands, he knelt at the base

---

39 AMDG represents the Latin words "Ad Majorem Dei Gloriam," meaning "for the greater glory of God." It is a Latin phrase which would have been taught to French children by the Jesuit missionaries.

of the tree, sticking one of the brands into the ground at each side of the tree but the taller of the three was placed directly in front. Bending forward at the waist until his face was upon the ground, he worshiped, repeating prayers as he could remember them. On this holy night,

Jean-Pierre sought to give honor to the Holy Christ here in the wilderness.

It was almost a week later when Jean-Pierre left the beech grove at the mouth of the valley. In that time, his knee had healed and all the extra bear meat had been dried over the cook fire. Also, the bear's hide had been tanned with its own brain, making it soft and pliable. It would protect the winter traveler from frigid weather by day as a cape or by night as a bedcover.

His intention now was to continue westward across the high, wooded tableland. Somewhere beyond, there were rivers which could take him southward to the Mississippi. Traveling with the travois was much easier with the gentle slope of the land. He knew that it would get lower as he traveled away from the ridge. It was during that day's travel that he came onto a large pond which had been cut out of the surface by an earlier action of water. The striking thing about the pond was the abundance of swans on the water, giving the pond's surface the appearance of deep snow.[40]

Jean-Pierre pushed on, taking advantage of traveling on the frozen ground. He knew that it would soften later when the weather warmed and travel would then be much slower. At times

---

40   This body of water was known by locals as "The Swan Pond." The pond existed into the mid-twentieth century and has now been drained, filled and turned into farm land. The area continues to bear the name "Swan Pond."

it was difficult to keep on course as changes of direction often had to be made due to sloughs or fallen trees. There was a great deal of evidence of the earthquake here though not nearly so much as in the Grand Marais. Occasionally, he would see a tree which had been too poorly rooted to withstand the shaking. The overcast sky also hindered his keeping to his westerly course as direction could not be acquired from the sun.

About mid-afternoon, Jean-Pierre came to the banks of a small river which flowed a southward course. He guessed this was the Riviere Cache, as he had been told by other Frenchmen that it was a minor river between the hilly ridge and the mountains in the west.[41] While stopping here for his noonday meal, he considered following it south, possibly using his axe to build a raft for easier travel. It was tempting, as by now the travois was becoming quite tiresome, especially in the soft soil of the bottomland. But on longer reflection, he decided to travel on westward to strike a larger water course. The Riviere Cache at this juncture was so crooked and choked with fallen trees that travel by raft would not be practical. By using one of these trees, Jean-Pierre was able to carry his supplies, furs, and travois to the western side.

The days had become heavily overcast with the warmer weather. Without the aid of the sun for direction, Jean-Pierre knew that he could not hold to a true westerly course. His intuition told him that he was veering somewhat to the north. It was another two

---

41   By the mid-twentieth century, only a few sections of the original river channel remained. Early in that century, the original Cache River was channelized in an effort to drain the vast bottomlands for farming. The Cache was particularly crooked and choked with fallen timber as it had not the water force to keep its channel clear. It originates near the Missouri line and empties into the White River at Clarendon, Arkansas, some 150 miles south.

days of slow traveling before he reached the larger stream he was quite sure was the Riviere Noire.[42] This was a river about fifty yards across with a free-flowing current. He was greatly relieved to have reached it as the travois had long ago become quite burdensome.

There was much old sign of many previous camps about, but none of them suited him.[43] Walking downstream, Jean-Pierre looked for a suitable place to camp as he would remain on the river's bank long enough to construct a raft. It would allow him to travel south with ease as opposed to slowly dragging the travois every foot of the way. Some distance downstream he found the camp situation he sought. It was an area of high land with some fallen timber nearby for his campfire. The river's bank was gently sloping where the raft might be assembled. Also, there were several small cypresses along the river's edge which would be suitable material for the raft.

Jean-Pierre made his camp against a large fallen cypress which had laid upon the dark woodland floor for many years. Its now horizontal trunk could serve him both as wind break and as heat reflector for his cook fire. He cut and trimmed some slender trees to frame a shelter, covering them with his canvas. Satisfied with his temporary camp, he set some lines out in the river for fresh fish, baiting them with pieces of dried meat. Also, the fish trap was lowered along one of the steeper banks. He had hopes of fresh fish

---

42 Noire (pronounced "nwar") in French means black. The Black River begins from the springs of the Ozark plateau in Missouri, flowing south into the White River near Newport, Arkansas. Through the alluvial bottomlands it picks up more soil content, taking on a dark color. In contrast, the White River, where joined by the Black, is still quite clear as it is fresh from the mountains.

43 This location had been a meeting ground between local Indians and French traders. The nearby community is named Delaplaine (of the plain).

by tomorrow morning. It was almost dark now, so a fire was lit with flint and striker and water was set on to boil. The river water from the Riviere Noire was quite clear, but it needed to be heated anyway to warm up his insides. There was no more coffee, so Jean-Pierre had to be content with boiling the sassafras roots that he had collected near his Christmas camp.

Into the night he sat on his cache of furs under the shelter, alternately watching the fire before him and the stars overhead. Again, he thought back to the Lewis and Clark expedition and regretted the missed opportunity. He had to console himself with the adventures that had come his way through the years.

Though tired, he sat up late into the night, oblivious to the cold. A shooting star passed overhead, and Jean-Pierre wondered at its significance. Indian traditions were full of beliefs about such events. Could it mean that something great was about to come into his life? Or could it be a reflection of his own life? He hoped not, as shooting stars lasted but a short while and he desired a long life. Already he had lived longer than some men he had known. He wasn't certain, but he thought that he should be about forty-nine years old, a long life by many standards. And he was by no means ready to end it now. Life was a joy for him to experience and share. The lure of the new trail or further horizon was always a draw upon him. The Arkansas land held many trails and rivers that he would like to explore while his health still permitted it. This was something to consider as he did not get about with as much vigor as he had when he was younger.

All the next day Jean-Pierre worked to assemble the basic structure of the raft he would use to carry him downstream toward the Fleuve Mississippi. First, he cut down three cypress trees about fifteen inches in diameter just above the base. From these, he cut six logs of fourteen-foot lengths. These were then rolled into position on the sloping bank of the river, each alongside the others. Tired from the exertion after the difficult journey with the travois, he quit his efforts a couple of hours before dark. With the catfish caught during the day, Jean-Pierre took a leisurely evening meal. Afterward, he strode along the river, choosing the small cypress he would cut the next day for the raft's floor. Much more tired this night, he slept early.

Early morning found him cutting down the small cypress chosen the evening before. These were approximately four inches in diameter. All were trimmed to seven-foot lengths and carried back to camp. It took several such trips before enough were gathered to build a floor over the six cypress logs. Strips of bark were peeled from young hickories for lashing the small logs together into a floor over the larger logs below. This was slow work, and he was not quite half finished when a late afternoon rain drove him to his camp.

Jean-Pierre retreated to his shelter to rekindle the fire for his evening meal. On one of his trips out to strip the hickory bark, he had found abundant sign of beaver in a nearby bayou. On a later trip, he had taken some of his traps and set them out. Now while water heated, he thought of those traps and hoped that right now old man beaver was coming to the bait. Sitting there alone before his fire in the vast river bottom, he reflected that this winter's trip already had been a remarkable experience. And in spite of the unsettling of the great earthquake and the forced change in direction, he had managed to trap a good number of furbearers. The winter still held promise and he believed that by the time he returned to St. Louis in the spring, this would prove to be one of his most successful trips.

More relaxed on this night than the ones past, Jean-Pierre settled down for sleep. Covered over by the bear robe and his fur cape, he was quite warm and quickly settled into a sound sleep.

After taking several fish from his lines and the trap early the next morning, Jean-Pierre cooked enough of the fish to start his day. Then he returned to the work of the raft to complete the weaving of the floor. It was slow work, requiring many trips into the woods to strip more bark from the young hickories. But with it completed, he felt somewhat freed from the restraints which the earthquake had brought upon him.

Satisfied that the floor poles would hold tight to the larger logs below, he now built a framework up from the floor to hold his canvas. This would give him a semi-permanent shelter without having to construct a new one each night. As there were no cedar here in the bottomland, the cache of furs was laid under the canvas to form his bed. For a fireplace, first, a bed of grass was forced in between the small logs of the floor. Then, sand was brought from the river's edge to cover the grass bed. The grass would keep the sand from falling through the logs and the sand would keep the logs from catching fire. All this was held together by a simple frame of short poles. Now Jean-Pierre could safely build a fire on board the raft. All his efforts so far on the raft would preclude his having to construct a fresh camp each night.

With his camp set upon the raft already, Jean-Pierre chose to move onto the raft even if he wasn't quite ready to quit the area. A long, stout oak pole had been reserved during the construction process to shove the raft off from the bank into the river. Now Jean-Pierre used this to lift and push until only the end of the raft was still in contact with the bank. A length of woven rawhide was used to secure the raft to a small tree.

The day was almost gone, and Jean-Pierre had one more thing he wanted to get done. With his bow in hand, he walked away from the camp with his long-legged gait. With purpose, he stepped in the direction of a well-used trail where the deer traveled down to the river for water. There was little need to worry about making noise as previous flooding had scoured the ground clean of any leaves. He knew just the place where he would have an advantage in spite of his weak bow. This place would allow him to shoot the bow from close range, hopefully making up for its lack of power.

Upon arriving near the trail, Jean-Pierre approached the butt of a large fallen white oak which had fallen across the deer trail. As it had fallen into another large tree, its trunk was held up from the trail, with its top projecting upward. His moccasined feet made no sound as he walked up its length. Jean-Pierre lightly stepped up the trunk, weaving himself around the limbs until he was beyond the trail and as high as the top would allow him to be without wavering under his weight. Here he turned around and sat, fixing his feet upon the bases of two outstretching limbs. From this position he could clearly see the trail ten feet below. This situation put him several feet above the deer's line of sight and would allow his scent to drift away unnoticed. He readied his hickory bow and one of the ash arrows and then waited without sound or motion. It was nearly dusk when Jean-Pierre detected movement from his right. Without any other motion, he shifted his eyes slightly to allow him to see in this direction. Coming along the trail was a doe.[44] She appeared to

---

44 Indians in the region preferred to kill a doe at this time of the winter. The bucks were thin and tough from their experiencing the rut while the does had more fat. Also, the unborn fawn they often carried was considered a delicacy.

be coming to the river for water, just as he had expected a deer to do at that time of day.

Careful now not to shift his weight for fear of causing the top to shake and give away his position, he watched her step in her slight way along the narrow path. As she began to step under the tree where his overhead position would not be noticeable, he eased up the bow and slowly drew back the string. He held the power of the bow until the doe stepped out from under the fallen oak. When his line of sight centered just behind her shoulder, he released the arrow. In the instant the arrow struck her, she sprang upward and bounded to the far side of the trail, coming to a stop a short distance away as she neither heard nor saw any pursuit. Here she stood as her life's blood drained away within her. In a few moments she collapsed. Jean-Pierre had watched all of this from his perch and was pleased that his Indian skill had again provided food for his camp. Descending the tree, he walked to the fallen doe and quickly from much practice opened the body cavity with his knife and removed the internal organs. The heart and liver were separated and later replaced in the body cavity. All four feet were then tied together with a heavy and wide strap of rawhide. Now Jean-Pierre could simply heft the carcass onto one of his shoulders and carry it back to his camp.

Later that evening Jean-Pierre lay upon his furs while looking over the fire toward the lower river. A cup of hot sassafras tea filled one hand and a pipe rested in the other. A full moon lit up the night, and the river's surface reflected its brilliance. The fresh deer carcass hung from a tripod of light poles on the front end of the raft and strips of the fresh tenderloin were suspended by green willow limbs over a bed of red hot coals. Sizzling sounds came from the fire as juices dropped to the coals below. The river current made a low and sluggish sound as it moved around the raft. An owl gave a distinctive hooting call in search of a mate.

This was a cherished part of Jean-Pierre's world, alone in the deep woods. Though it was true that he enjoyed the company of the French villages as well as those of the Indian tribes, he mostly preferred his time alone in the woods. He had two distinct natures; one gregarious needing companionship with laughter and stories, and one of withdrawal needing the solitude of the wilderness. He would alternate between the two, satisfying his social appetites as they came and went. Now, he needed to be away from other people. He sensed that this need arose from his desire to revisit the memories of his parents. And here in the deep woods was the best place that could be done.

He thought of them now as he began to eat the sweet, tender strips of venison. He chewed slowly, remembering some of the camps and trips that the three of them had enjoyed together. At times like this he often asked himself why he had not taken a wife and possibly enjoyed the companionship as had his father. There were several women over the years who had caught his eye, some French and some Indian. And there had been matchmaking friends who had tried to help the process.

The French women had always been the daughter of a farmer or shopkeeper and all had been strongly tied to village life. None of them would have been happy as the wife of a trapper and trader like himself. He was very much like the famed French voyageur in that his frequent and long travels was not the life for most women. With the Indian women, it seemed that he held such a high standard from the memory of his mother that none of them measured up. At any rate, the painful memories caused him to be afraid of losing a wife on the trail and re-entering the path of sorrow.

Jean-Pierre remained in the area of his first contact with the Riviere Noire for several more days as the opportunities for furs were good. Having constructed the raft, he could now access the far bank without soaking himself in the chilly waters. The Noire was the largest river he had encountered since leaving the Mississippi at Ste. Genevieve.

When the furs began to diminish, he pushed the raft out into the current to allow it to drift downriver. Jean-Pierre wasn't sure of his direction as the day was heavily overcast, but believed the course to be more westerly than south at this point. Late that day a secondary watercourse entered from the north.[45]

This new river was smaller though not appreciably so, and brought water much clearer than that of the Noire. Jean-Pierre would have liked to have gone upstream. However, a raft was poorly suited for going against a current, and the current of this new river was noticeably stronger than that of the Noire.

With some effort, he navigated the bulky raft over to the north bank. There he secured it to a small tree. Hopeful of catching more beaver, Jean-Pierre worked his way through the dense woods, carrying some traps over his left shoulder and hefting his lance in his right hand. For the remaining hour of good light, he searched in vain for small bayous or sloughs where beaver might reside. Unable to locate any at all, he retraced his steps to the raft in the fading light. Without any reason to remain, Jean-Pierre released the raft

45   The Current River flows out of the hilly region of Missouri, having clear fast water to dump into the more sluggish Black River.

in the next morning's first light to continue downstream. About mid-day he observed another river entering the Noire from the north. This one was much smaller than the one previous and did not have nearly as much current.[46]

Again hopeful for furs, Jean-Pierre pushed hard against the rudder pole, forcing the raft into the juncture of the currents. The stronger current of the Noire carried the raft against the far north bank. Here he tied off and again walked upstream in search of beaver. This time he had success as the slowness of this small river was much more suited to the habitat of the beaver. He set out all his traps before giving attention to finding fresh meat for his cook fire. Throughout the afternoon Jean-Pierre walked a circuitous course through the river bottom back to his raft. The area was mostly tall timber, interspersed with cane brakes and sloughs of earlier water courses. He found no opportunities for deer though there were plentiful sign. His arrows had connected with one large rabbit, common to this great bottomland. He had first seen them upon entering the Grand Marais. On the average, they were about three times the size of the rabbits he had commonly seen in the highlands farther north or upon crossing the ridge.[47] While he still had his fusil he had shot several of them. Since the earthquake, he had managed to snare one during his arduous journey across the bottomland west of the highland ridge. It occurred to him now that he had not noticed any of these large rabbits along either side of the ridge, but only in

---

46 The Fourche enters the Black River shortly after the Current, just to the northeast of Pocahontas, Arkansas. It is a small mountain stream, no more than fifty miles in length. The word means "fork" or "branch" in French and is pronounced "foorsh."

47 These large rabbits are commonly called swamp rabbits, growing to about five pounds. The inhabit the Southern bottomland.

the bottomland.

Jean-Pierre trapped along this small river for a week before giving it up to float on downstream. There had been severe tremors during the night, causing him to become once again unsettled. Besides, Jean-Pierre felt it was time to leave anyway. He had taken several beaver as well as raccoon and mink during his short stay. He regretted not having a pirogue to explore the river farther upstream. It was after leaving the mouth of the small river that Jean-Pierre began to see hills on the west side of the Riviere Noire. He determined that this must be the eastern edge of the mountains about which he had heard so much from other French traders. Again he wished for a pirogue as the raft would never traverse the swift-flowing bayous which would surely flow out of the mountains. Two days later as the Riviere Noire was maintaining a southerly course, he discovered a small French settlement along the right bank of the river. With joy, he tied off his raft at their landing and approached the cabins. A lone woman came hesitantly to a doorway.

"Bonjour, Madame," called out Jean-Pierre.

A smile came upon her face and she replied with, "Bonjour Monsieur, entrez, sil vous, plait."

Jean-Pierre was overjoyed at finding some of his countrymen as he needed a respite from the isolation. But, he became guarded as he saw no men about. Upon inquiry, he learned that all the men and the other women were off on a hunting trip. He visited with her at some length, savoring every word of the exchange with another person. But, out of respect for this woman, he declined staying, stating that he was a hurry to get downriver. As he pushed off the raft, he held great regret for the men's absence as he needed both companionship and an opportunity to trade for some much needed articles.[48]

Shortly after leaving the small French settlement, he saw another river, this one coming from the west. This river was small in size, but brought into the Riviere Noire a strong current, clear to the gaze and cool to the touch. In spite of the considerable tremors over the previous days, Jean-Pierre tied up his raft on the west bank of the Noire and walked up the mountain stream as he had on previous occasions. Some distance upstream he found another mountain river joining the first, this one flowing from the north. He took some time to investigate. Dense canebrakes and old sloughs were scattered along the valley floor. All through this area Jean-Pierre found little fur bearing game. He determined that the local settlers had already trapped out the area.[49]

In this manner Jean-Pierre worked his way south down the Riviere Noire, stopping for several days wherever fur bearing animals were numerous. He began to note that there were no bayous of consequence entering the river from the east. There the vast timbered bottomland stretched for many miles. But the western bank was broken at regular intervals by bayous or rivers of some consequence. All of these were investigated for the purpose of trapping, steadily adding to Jean-Pierre's stock of furs. He took so many furs in these days that he made little progress downriver.

---

48 Many Arkansans are familiar with the early American settlement of Davidsonville along the Black River, just to the north of present Black Rock, Arkansas. It was the site of Arkansas' first post office in 1817 and is now a state park. This settlement was first occupied by Frenchmen who sold their improvements to the American settlers who came later.

49 At this juncture, Spring River flows into the Black from the northwest, just north of Black Rock, Arkansas. A short distance up the Spring, it is joined by the Eleven Point River which flows from the north. Both rivers are mountain streams of cold, clear water.

By now he had furs of a large variety of animals, tied in neat bundles with strips of rawhide. He had hides of deer, beaver, mink, raccoon, and opossum. Also, he had the one bear hide he had taken after crossing the high ridge. That hide, in particular, formed a vital part of his bed covering to ward off the intense cold of the winter nights.

He had the raft floating downstream one morning when a shock of great violence shook everything about him.[50] The river convulsed as if affected by a tide and the trees all about waved and trembled like tall grass in a wind. Some of the weaker ones actually fell to the ground or into the river. At any instant, he feared that a tree would fall across his raft. Jean-Pierre knew little of earthquakes but was certain that this one was almost as unsettling as the original one back in the Grand Marais over a month ago. With all the speed available to a raft, Jean-Pierre poled his way downstream in another effort to distance himself from the danger behind him. On through the day he kept up his pace, accelerated all the more by another violent shock just after noon.

During the days following, Jean-Pierre trapped little, but persisted in forcing the raft down the river. Out of fear of the quakes which seemed to come from behind him, he took to traveling at night as the moon gave enough light to navigate the river. His progress was often halted by a fallen tree across part of the river. Even these obstacles did not detain him. At this point, more furs were a secondary concern to the violent quakes. Shocks and tremors, some of which were quite violent, occurred daily. Though he and the raft sustained no damage, the numerous aftershocks kept him nervous.

---

50 This earthquake was the second "great" earthquake and occurred on 25 January 1812.

He passed several small settlements during these nights, but forsook any opportunity for trade to get away from the shocks.[51]

Two weeks after the second large quake, he was beginning to be his calm jovial self and relax with the motion of the river when another quake struck, this time in the latter part of the night. The raft was tied off, and Jean-Pierre was still sleeping. His entire camp shook so that he rolled from his bed and almost into the river. Hanging on tightly, he thought he felt the raft being lifted from the river itself. In the starlight, he could see the tops of the timber shaking violently. Snapping, popping and tearing sounds came from throughout the timber. He knew that trees, large and small, were being torn apart as they stood and were falling in all directions. Through the remainder of the night he lay nervous in his bed as the earth was in continual motion.[52]

At the first break of dawn, Jean-Pierre untied the raft and eagerly pushed it into the current. But his progress was slow that day as the river was sometimes choked with fallen trees and other wood debris. His efforts were stimulated in that tremors continued all through the day, giving a time of quietness of not more than a very few minutes.

In the days ahead, neither the rains nor the cold fronts induced him to remain at one place longer than a night's stay. Nor did he

---

51 Several small French settlements existed along the Black and White rivers in the early 1800's. At this point in his journey, our fictional character would have passed in the night Portia, Lauratown, and Clover Bend. This French population had been displaced from the southern Illinois region by American settlers some years previous.

52 This third and last of the great earthquakes occurred about 3:00 AM on 7 February. It was considered by all eyewitness reports as being as powerful if not more so than the first one on 16 December. Tremors continued in the region throughout all of 1812.

pursue any furs. Day after day he worked the raft down the current and around numerous fallen trees. After some time, he determined that he had distanced himself far enough from the Grand Marais that there was little actual danger from the shocks. From the day he had pushed the raft off into the current of the Riviere Noire, six weeks had elapsed before Jean-Pierre came onto another river of similar size and volume. It also joined the Noire from the west. At this juncture, bottomland surrounded both rivers. Jean-Pierre was not able to see the highlands to the west. But he deduced that the mountains were not very far to the west as the new river was quite clear and its current was much stronger than that of the Noire. Again drawing upon the wealth of knowledge possessed by the typical French trapper, he determined that this new river must be the Riviere Blanche.[53] He had been told that it drew its origin from far in the western mountains and that it was the major waterway through those mountains.

Unable to work his raft up the oncoming current, Jean-Pierre used the rudder to shift closer to the west bank. Instead of tying at the first opportunity as had been his custom over the past several weeks, he allowed the raft to ease its way downstream. All the while he looked for a suitable long-term campsite on the west bank. At a point where the river had swerved around a large bend, sand had been deposited inside the bend to form a clean white bar with no mud or brush. Here he guided the raft onto the bar. With a long rope of woven hickory bark, he tied it to an overhanging willow.

---

53 Blanche is a French word, meaning white, pure, or clean. It is pronounced "blawnsh." The Black River joins the White River, a particularly clear mountain river of some consequence, near Newport, Arkansas. The White continues on south and east to enter the Mississippi just a few miles north of the mouth of the Arkansas River.

With intentions of remaining in this area for a longer time than most of his camps, Jean-Pierre set about cutting up a large supply of driftwood for his fire.

Here, he intended to sleep on the sand bar, as the cramped quarters of the raft were beginning to pain him. The weather had warmed over the last few days, bringing relief from the frequent ice and sleet storms of the past weeks. A warming sun beat upon him as he set up a camp on the sand bar.

CHAPTER FOUR

Hoosiers

WITH HIS CAMP SET UP ON THE RIVIERE BLANCHE, Jean-Pierre took certain precautions. He had traveled the trails and waterways of the back woods his entire life and had developed rules of life just as a person from a city. In the weeks of travel since the earthquake, his chance of meeting another person had been very remote. Now he had every possibility of encountering other people, either French trappers like himself, Indians, or American settlers. The settlements he had passed in the night were evidence of this.

Though he now wanted to encounter other travelers, he understood that some of them could be dangerous. While white travelers too often looked upon the chance encounter with Indians as being dangerous, his father and mother had taught him that most danger lay in other white people. Wild and dangerous men had fled here beyond the limits of established society to avoid the workings of justice. Bands of these thieves and murderers often lived along the wilderness routes where they might waylay the passing traveler. Because frontier justice could be swift and severe, the victim of even a robbery would often be murdered to leave no witness.

By now Jean-Pierre had been alone long enough to kindle a strong desire for human companionship. Other people also brought the possibility of replenishing the items which had been lost during the first earthquake. And, he was anxious for news from the Fleuve Mississippi. He particularly wanted to hear how the French settlements had fared during the three earthquakes.

Not knowing the kind of men he would encounter, Jean-Pierre took certain steps to protect his winter's work. He hauled almost all his furs out into the woods away from the river channel and found a hiding place. The cache site was a fallen hollow tree. After working to remove more of the soft punky inner wood, he pushed the bales of furs far into the recess of the hollow and plugged the opening with larger pieces of the punk. This punk was then doused with the urine he had saved from the bear. He had stored the urine in a small gourd for just such an occasion. Hopefully, its pungent odor would convince other animals of the presence of a bear inside the hollow log. Before leaving, Jean-Pierre covered the opening and the immediate area with a careful collection of brush which would not only conceal the cache but also would discourage any traveler from walking near the opening.

He kept a few furs, mostly of inferior quality, at the camp. These would both mask the possibility of a larger cache in the area as well as give him something of trading value when he did encounter a French or American traveler. Game in the area was still plentiful though he was sure that both French and Americans had worked this area before. He saw lots of bear sign in the cane brakes west of the river. Again, he regretted losing his fusil during the earthquake. Bear hides were of great value and the oil rendered from their fat was worth even more.

His camp was in plain sight on the sand bar to announce his presence should anyone happen along in his absence. Jean-Pierre had been at this camp for about a week when someone finally came along. He had been resting in camp about midday when he noticed a heron disturbed from its perch downriver. Looking toward the disturbance, he caught sight of a pirogue rounding the downstream bend. Quietly he sat on the sand and smoked his pipe. He did not want to give the appearance of being overly anxious and foolish, possibly tempting an unscrupulous person to take advantage of him. The question came to him as to whether these men had any tobacco and how difficult it might be for him to trade for some. At present, he was smoking shredded up grape vines, as his supply of tobacco had run out several days before.

As the pirogue drew near, the two occupants changed their expression from that of concern to one of interest. The forward man was about the age of Jean-Pierre with a heavily weathered face and a stooped posture. The man in the rear was quite young, possibly a son as Jean-Pierre noted a facial resemblance. Both men were dressed in moccasins, buckskin leggings, loin cloth, and homespun shirts.[54]

It was the older man who called out a greeting. "Hallo the camp, mind some comp'ny?" Using his pipe hand, Jean-Pierre waved them on toward the bank, extending the greeting to stop and share his camp. Guiding their craft alongside the raft, they disembarked, all the while expressing surprise at the presence of his camp.

"Howdy, Frenchy," spoke the older man as he recognized from Jean-Pierre's clothing that he was of French heritage. Jean-Pierre showed no offense at what he considered a negative reference to his people. "Been camped here long, hev ya? M'name's Zeke Talbot an' dis her's m' boy William. Him and me've been down to the Post doin' some tradin'. Been gone ser'vral weeks now. Anxious to git on home up the White and check on the wife and other young 'uns."

---

54   It was common for frontiersmen to adopt the dress of the Indian.

Responding in a broken English that he felt was expected of him, Jean-Pierre stated, "Non, Monsieur, only a few days here. Jean-Pierre has been waiting upon such a kind gentleman as yourself to come along and render aid. I took a terrible loss during the earthquakes this winter. I very much could use some items before continuing on down the Riviere Blanch. You trade, yes?"

"Depends," replied the older American. "We've not got much, jes' scratchin' out a life here from the woods. But we'll pro'bly find som'thin' useful to ya. Jes' whut ya got fer tradin'?"

"Only a few furs, Monsieur, but I would gladly trade them all for some supplies if you could spare them," stated Jean-Pierre.

"Shore, Frenchy, we's could do som' tradin', glad to hep out, whut say ya gather up your outfit, sech as it is and com' on upriver to our settlement. We'll uncork a jug and loosen up 'fore the tradin'," replied the American.

"Oui, Monsieur, merci," answered Jean-Pierre, still maintaining the broken English and French which he believed more profitable for the time. Quickly he gathered his few possessions and stowed them in the middle of the American's dugout.

Most of Jean-Pierre's outfit drew no notice, but when he picked up his lance, the son's eyes became fixed upon it. As the son sat mute, the father remarked, "don't you hev' a rifle, or even a musket, Frenchy?"

"Non, monsieur, it was lost in the shaking of the earth, swallowed up as I almost was," responded Jean-Pierre.

"But," interjected the American, "ya' mean ya' been gettin' along with no more than thet thar spear?"

Allowing his own eyes to take in the well shaped and decorated lance, Jean-Pierre stated, "it is not the weapon, monsieur, but the hand. In my hand, it was enough for a bear in his den." With this flat statement, he fingered the long black claws which hung from his neck.

With a deep sense of awe, Zeke Talbot slowly said, "Now, 'fore we leave, we'd best take the time to tuck away thet thar' raft of yourn or else some river pirate might make offen wi'it. Thar's an old channel downriver a short ways whar we kin stick it out of sight of the main river." With help from the two settlers, Jean-Pierre's raft was secreted away from possible theft or destruction for the duration of his visit with them. Jean-Pierre appreciated their offering to secure his only means of transportation. He took this as a sign of honest men.

It was after nightfall when the Talbots guided the pirogue to the bank beside a rough clearing. By the light of the rising moon, Jean-Pierre could see two log structures which were set away from the river on a piece of high land. Smoke came from the top of one, so he determined that to be their cabin. As they disembarked, dogs rushed out from the structures to bark and howl. This warning and challenge continued until the dogs discovered that the landing party was the master of the house. The all looked upon Jean-Pierre with suspicion, some actually walking up stiff-legged to sniff his leggings. The three men unloaded the pirogue. Jean-Pierre could carry his few possessions by himself, but the Talbot's cargo required several trips. Everything was carried first into a makeshift barn with only a few of the Talbot's items carried on into the cabin.

By moonlight, Jean-Pierre examined the surroundings. Household items and implements were strewn about with no order. And, even in the limited light, he could see that the workmanship of the barn was crude at best. But it would give the livestock some shelter from the wind and rain. As they approached the cabin, he noted the same crudeness in construction. He was accustomed to the French houses built with much more care. He could see that there was little material separating the outside from the inside at the gables. The long streaks of light visible between the logs showed that little effort had been given to chinking. He could see enough light through the roof that he wondered how it would keep out a heavy rain. And, of course, on a cold night it would hold little warmth inside.

He walked into the cabin behind the Talbots to Zeke and William's reunion with the family after their several weeks of absence. He had already noted that no one had come out of the house to greet them at the river or to help unload the pirogue.

Jean-Pierre stood now just inside the door which he had closed behind himself. He waited patiently for some introduction. At first, it was as if he were not there at all. The family was involved in the gala time of greetings now that the men were inside the cabin.

Jean-Pierre took this time to look around the cabin. It was a one-room structure as was common along the frontier. The large fireplace stretched almost the length of one end wall, its wooden frame covered over inside with fire dried clay. Another door stood directly opposite the one they had just entered. This possibly relieved some congestion with the several children. But another reason was scratched out on the dirt floor between the doors. Here a series of scars in the hard packed soil reached from door to door. These marks and the wide width of the doors suggested the common practice of using one of the family oxen to drag logs into the cabin, with the oxen walking on out the other door once unhitched from the log. This log could then be used as a bench for the children or visitors until it was needed to bank the night fire. Then it would simply be rolled into the fireplace whole.

It was evident that every piece of furniture was hand-made, from chairs and stools to the table and lamp stands. Each piece was simply taken from a tree and crudely shaped into the use needed by the family. It was apparent that few tools and little skill had been used to make them. The family table was made of puncheon or split logs, roughly pegged together. The many children were apparently accommodated at the table by a split log bench, supported by four stout poles shortened to the right height for an adult. The children's legs would, of course, dangle. Candle stands were flattened pegs driven into augered out holes in the log walls. Hooks for clothing and tools, kitchen or otherwise, were secured in like fashion, though there was not a great deal of either clothing or tools to be seen.

On each side of the fireplace, deerskin bags hung from the roof timbers. These bags were skins that had been scraped clean of hair and resewn somewhat to the original shape of the animal. From experience and a knowing eye, Jean-Pierre gathered that one was filled with honey and the other with bear oil. The bear oil was considered a necessity by all frontier families, while the honey was a lavish luxury in a land of deprivations. Both items were also easily sold or traded for shipment to Nouvelle Orleans.[55]

---

55   The fat was taken from a bear carcass and rendered down into an oil which was used for cooking oil, medicine, body lotion, lamp oil, lubricant for rifle balls, and several other uses. In the region where the White and Black rivers join, there was a particularly high concentration of bears. There the taking of bears for their oil later became a thriving trade. Hollowed out logs, much like dugout canoes or watering troughs, were used to hold the oil for shipment. A wide plank was used to cap the container. In this manner, the oil troughs were loaded onto steamboats for shipment downriver. Oil Trough, Arkansas, a community in this region, received its name from this trade.

A quick glance upward showed a loft on the opposite end of the cabin from the fireplace, apparently for the younger children. Access was not by steps or even a ladder but by crude toe holds chopped into a leaning pole. Certainly any child growing up in such a house would quickly develop agility and strength.

The family finished their salutary conversations and, one by one, began to eye the stranger up and down. It struck Jean-Pierre that this greeting was much like the one given him earlier by the family dogs, particularly when one of the smaller children, a little girl, came up to him and took hold of the legging of his left leg and tugged as if to see if he were real. Jean-Pierre then knelt to her level and greeted her with his wide smile and flashing eyes. She quickly smiled in return, holding up both hands as if to hide her face.

At this point, Zeke Talbot spoke in reference to Jean-Pierre, "This her's a Frenchy we picked up offen a sand bar jes b'low whar the Black joins up wi' the White. Says he lost most of his outfit back in the big quake over ta th' east of th' ridge. Figures to do som' tradin' wi' us 'fore workin' his way on down to the Miss'sippi." With this speech of introduction over, Zeke Talbot eased himself into a much-worn rocking chair near the fireplace, muttering something about it being good to be home. Somewhat eased by an explanation of Jean-Pierre's presence, the family as one turned toward the fire and continued talking about the men's trip down the Riviere

Honey bees were a European contribution to the North American scene. They spread rapidly west ahead of the American settlers. The honey was considered a great treat, so much so that hunters would sometimes gorge themselves on it when given the opportunity. It was collected like bear oil, contained in skin bags, to be later traded for items which they could not manufacture themselves. Honey, along with bear oil, would be shipped downriver to Nouvelle Orleans where it would be loaded on ocean-going vessels.

Blanche to Post aux Arkansas.

Jean-Pierre took this as his cue and stepped toward the warmth of the fireplace, taking a seat on the wood pile off in one corner. Here he observed this backwoods family. Certainly he had grown up on the frontier much as they had. The difference in his experience was that his family routinely visited one of the French settlements along the Fleuve Mississippi. There he was exposed to well-built houses clustered in a settlement with a tightly-knit social system of religion, tradesmen, peddlers, and farmers. Community customs dictated adherence to some standard of education, religion, clothing, cleanliness, and manners. Here, this family was so isolated from others that laxness was their byword. There was no one to challenge or stimulate them to improve or even to maintain any standard of civilized communities. Jean-Pierre had seen this situation all across the frontiers of Tennessee, Kentucky, Indiana, Ohio, and Missouri.[56]

He knew by this time that the Talbots would do little more

---

56 A caste of people populated the frontier of the Mississippi Valley who were in reality much less civilized than the Indian they followed. They were, by and large, an unkempt, dirty uneducated, and unmannered group of people who had a strong aversion to civilized society. Typically they entered the frontier to throw up a crude dwelling and take their livelihood from the game in the woods. Other than their gardening, their only effort at farming would be for their own needs of corn for eating or making whiskey. It would not enter their minds to raise corn to sell. Also, they only occupied the land until permanent settlers moved into the area. Often they would sell their "improvement" for a few dollars before moving farther back into the woods to begin again. In the Ohio and Mississippi River valleys, these people were known as "Hoosiers." The origin of the term is unknown, but it seems to have been applied to frontiersmen moving from Kentucky. Some men might look down upon them, but they did perform a valuable function in the opening of the frontier, as they took some of the starch out of the wilderness. They were people of great self-reliance and resourcefulness, needing little of others.

with their land in the future than they had done in the four years they had lived here. They were essentially hunters, living off what could easily be taken from the land. He had seen Americans like this many times in his travels. But tonight Jean-Pierre was glad to share their company. After many weeks alone in the backwoods, he was eager for human companionship.

Shortly after finding his rocker, Zeke Talbot called to one of the girls, one about fourteen years of age, "Rachel, fetch yore paw the jug, gurl." This he uncorked and from it took a long draw before lowering it to catch his breath. "Ah, no whiskey is like home grown," he declared. With this, he passed it to Jean-Pierre. Jean-Pierre took the jug with hearty thanks and also took a short draw before passing it back. Though he appreciated their hospitality, he had never taken to the raw taste of American home-made whiskey. Throughout the evening, the jug passed around the room with all the adults sharing.

In like fashion the tobacco was passed. Zeke and William chewed theirs while Mrs. Talbot and the oldest daughter, Emily, each smoked a pipe. Jean-Pierre had found pipe smoking common among women and girls in the American settlements. Of course, he preferred his pipe.

Zeke told stories about the trip downriver to Poste aux Arkansas. But the big topic of the night was the earthquakes and the recurring almost daily aftershocks. The Talbots were eager to tell Jean-Pierre of their own experience here on the Riviere Blanche. When the first quake occurred, the whole family had run outside into the cold night air, afraid that their cabin would collapse. There they had huddled around a fire the rest of the night. The large after-shock about daylight rekindled their fears. They had continued sleeping outside by a fire for almost a week until they believed it might be safe enough inside the cabin. But the second and third quakes had terrified them all over again. They were by nature superstitious folk and such occurrences as the very earth shaking beneath their feet had unsettled them greatly.

Knowing that the shocks had come from the east, they were eager for Jean-Pierre to tell his story and wanted every detail. They had heard bits of news from river travelers, but this guest had been in the very heart of the upheaval. Jean-Pierre saw this as an opportunity to use his special gift as a storyteller to help him be accepted into this Hoosier family.

He told how he had been trapping his way down the Riviere St. Francois when the first great quake occurred, about the hut collapsing upon him, the horrible death of his pack horse, and of the waters spreading over the whole bottomland. Then they insisted he tell the details of his escape and how he had gotten out of the Grand Marais without a horse or a firearm. With the skills of a master storyteller, Jean-Pierre told what it was like that fateful night along the Riviere St. Francois with the earth shaking below him and trees falling over him. He emphasized his isolation, his fear, and his desperation. He told with great detail the building and the use of the travois, the lance, and the raft. The killing of the bear was brought out as the high point of it all. To add to the effect, he then lifted the bear claw necklace from out of his shirt for all the Talbots to see.

As he recounted these events, the children sat before the fire in their long buckskin shirts with large eyes and open mouths. The older children and adults were almost as spellbound. Jean-Pierre had told his story with great emotion, gestures of the hand, suspended pauses, and the raising and lowering of the voice. Each of the Talbots had hung on his every word.

When he signaled his finish by refilling his pipe and sitting back from the light, the smaller children drew closer to their mother. The older children pulled their clothes about them in some gesture of security.

Mrs. Talbot with a light voice said, "Wal, who'd a thought thet a fellar could'a got outen' of a fix like thet."

Williams expounded a "Whooee!"

Zeke Talbot added, "Sech a tale, I've never heerd the like, naw, siree." At this time, he determined it was time for another passing of the jug as the story seemed to have justified it.

Zeke Talbot began to add other stories from their trip. He spoke without the control or flourish of Jean-Pierre, and now seemed uncomfortably aware of it. But he continued on as the liquor was by now his driving force. He recounted stories he and William had heard while at Poste aux Arkansas. Someone there had told of an entire island on the Mississippi settling into the river, taking down a band of river pirates. Others had told of how upriver, near New Madrid, the river bottom separated in two different locations creating temporary waterfalls across the great river. There also had been stories of flatboats being pitched out of the river and of the entire river being jammed with logs and fallen trees. Apparently, the entire Mississippi Valley was shaken by the earthquake.

Jean-Pierre listened to these stories with deep concern for his friends in the French villages but knew that there was nothing he could do for them now. Whatever was done, was done. When he was able to return, he could then inquire as to their welfare.

He sat on the woodpile until the family slowly began to drift off to their beds. There were no above-ground beds, only pallets stuffed with corn shucks. As he watched them, he noted where different ones of the family settled for the night. Zeke and his wife laid themselves on a thick pallet in the far corner of the cabin. The youngest child, not yet away from his mother's breast, had already been laid upon it. Two girls, probably in their mid-teens, lifted their pallet off a wall and settled onto it on the same end as their parents. Williams and another one of the older boys laid themselves onto the dirt floor, separated from it only by a buffalo hide. Another buffalo robe provided a covering. All the smaller children scrambled up into the lofts.

Jean-Pierre followed William and the other boy, choosing the side near the wall for himself, to not make any of the family, particularly the womenfolk, nervous about his presence. Here he lay for several minutes, stimulated by the newness of the experience. Before sleep came to him, heavy breathing and snoring seemed to come from every corner of the cabin. With this, he also slept, his first experience in a house with a family since early last fall back in Ste. Genevieve.

The next morning Jean-Pierre awoke even earlier than usual. He wanted to be out of the cabin before the womenfolk awoke, as he felt it would make them more comfortable as they arose. But he did take the time to stir the coals in the fireplace and add several small pieces of wood to begin the day's fire. He knew that this simple chore would dispel the morning's chill and make meal preparation quicker for the cook. With this courtesy performed, he stepped out into the dawn of a new day.

Standing in front of the cabin for a few moments, he surveyed the frosty clearing, which would probably measure about four acres.

It was still rough as few stumps had been removed. Most trees had been chopped off at about twelve inches above the ground. A plow had evidently been worked around the stumps in years past to ready the soil for corn planting. A low rail fence enclosed the corn field. Some of last year's corn stalks still stood, but most had been eaten by the livestock.

Walking over to the barn area, Jean-Pierre looked over the Talbot livestock. They had two oxen, one milk cow, and three horses, none of which held an excess of fat. As there was no hay stored anywhere in sight, he assumed that the stock grazed about at will in the bottoms, getting feed where they could find it. By now the family dogs had discovered his presence. But this morning they showed little interest in him. Likely as he now held the scents of the cabin, identifying him as one of the household.

Walking out to the river bank, he sat down on a log. He filled his pipe with the fresh tobacco Zeke Talbot had given him last evening. It certainly was a pleasure to enjoy real tobacco again instead of the shredded grape vines he had been smoking the past few weeks.

He slowly experienced the satisfaction of his pipe with real tobacco as he sat and watched the river before him. The current seemed quite strong on this Riviere Blanche. He guessed the width of the river to be over fifty yards. Mallards were winging their way along the channel this morning, at times close enough for him to hear the beat of their wings. Their steady quacking filled the air in the moment of their passing. Jean-Pierre would have liked to have a fowling piece in his hand as roasted duck made a tasty dinner.[57] But

---

57 A fowling piece was an early shotgun, having a much thinner barrel wall than a rifle. As the name implies, it was designed primarily for

in lieu of that, he sat and enjoyed watching them pass.

From time to time pieces of driftwood floated by, causing Jean-Pierre to wonder what the upper part of this river held for a trapper such as himself. After a time his attention was drawn to the two pirogues on the bank. The larger craft was the one used by the Talbots to make their trading journey to Poste aux Arkansas. It was probably eighteen feet in length and was wide enough at the beam to hold a sizeable cargo. The smaller one was narrow and only about twelve feet long, obviously a craft more suited for one or two men traveling smaller bayous or working up the stronger currents. Jean-Pierre noted with some satisfaction that both pirogues were hewn from cypress logs by a highly skilled hand. He knew that cypress wood was light and very resistant to rot. Inside and out they both had a smooth, clean shape. No spot in the walls showed to be overly thin or heavy.

An idea began to form in his mind, one that gave him hope of better navigation for the remainder of his time on the Riviere Blanche and his return to Ste. Genevieve. He would have to carry it out with the deftness of a trading Frenchman. The thought of it brought a smile to his lips.

By this time sounds from the cabin indicated the Talbot family had begun their day. Presently, the adults and children, in turn, left the cabin to relieve themselves after their night's sleep. Jean-Pierre kept his watch upon the river, giving no notice of them.

After a time, William walked out to Jean-Pierre, bearing a cup of hot coffee. "Ma sed to brang this to ya', thought ya might enjoy it furst than in the mawnin', also sed she 'preciated yor' gittin' the far goin' 'for she got up," stated William with the most words

---

shooting small shot as opposed to a single ball.

Jean-Pierre had heard him speak at one time.

"Merci beaucoup, an' Jean-Pierre with thanking your kind mother also," replied Jean-Pierre. The fresh hot coffee tasted quite delicious on this frosty morning. Now he began implementing his idea. "Monsieur Williams, I have noticed the fine craftsmanship of your pirogues here. Could I ask who was the craftsman who worked them from the log?"

With some hesitation and a downward glance, Williams answered, "Uh, wal, ...I done these here dugouts myself. I don't rightly know what a craftsman might be. But Pa says I do a right good job."

"Ah, you yourself then, I compliment you on such works of art and beauty. The better work I have never seen before," spoke Jean-Pierre with an excited voice. "If I only owned such a craft myself, my travels would be so much the easier. The raft is so slow and cumbersome. And I cannot take it upstream against the current."

A loud, rough voice came then from the cabin, "Ya'll com' on and git yore breakfast, least what we've got." It was Zeke Talbot giving notice that the morning meal had been prepared. It proved to be simply a hot corn meal mush with broiled strips of salted bear ham.

After breakfast was over, the men stepped out into the morning sunshine and sat upon blocks at the woodpile. From behind them, Jean-Pierre heard Mrs. Talbot direct the two older girls to grind some corn for the day's use.

The girls walked to the barn where they each collected an arm load of corn ears still in the shuck. These they deposited beside a log out from the cabin where it was obvious this chore had been done before. The two girls sat on the log while they stripped off the shucks and shelled the kernels of corn off the cob with the heel of one hand, holding it with the other. The kernels fell into a bucket which sat on the ground between them. When this part was done, Rachel carried the bucket to a nearby stump hollowed out for grinding corn. She then poured the kernels into the hollow stump. Emily took hold of a small log which hung above the stump. The rope attached to the upper end of the log was tied to a springy hickory pole which leaned up from the ground. The log could be worked up and down into the hollow stump, with the pole doing its share of the lifting. But even with the help of the pole, it was still hard work. After a time of pounding the pestle into the stump, the corn was ground and could be used for various types of corn bread or cereal. It was then scooped out by hand and carried in the bucket to the cabin.

All this time Jean-Pierre continued his plan by heaping praise upon the craftsmanship of young William, making even the father proud. Considering that the Talbots were now in a mood to trade, Jean-Pierre began making offers of his peltries[58] for those items he deemed essential for his continued journey.

Jean-Pierre asked, "Monsieur Talbot, there is much need of a gun on the trail. Do you have one which you would consider trading?"

"Shore, Frenchy," answered Zeke Talbot, "Tyler," he called to one of the younger boys, "fetch me thet extry musket from the corner."

The boy trotted into the cabin and returned shortly with an

---

58 Peltry was a term for the hide or fur of a beaver. In a region where there was almost no money, a beaver pelt was a standard of trade accepted anywhere.

ancient and rusty musket.[59] Taking it from the boy, Zeke offered it to his guest, saying, "This'n is a mite old, but a straight shooter all the same," extending the weapon to his guest.

As Jean-Pierre examined the musket, Zeke Talbot set his firm price as he knew that there was not likely another firearm to be gained within two hundred miles. "Tell ye what I'll do, Frenchy, jes' cause I like ye, I'll take a dozen beaver for it, but not a one less."

Jean-Pierre gave it a careful examination. The firearm was indeed ancient and in a very poor state of care. Rust covered it from end to end and cracks showed not only in the stock, but in the hammer and lock as well. Silently he dismissed any possibility of the firearm being reliable.

Trying to hide his disappointment, Jean-Pierre replied, "Non, Monsieur, it is certainly a fine musket but I do not have so many beaver peltries that I can make the trade. Perhaps I could make trade for other things instead. Some corn meal would be greatly appreciated and possibly some salt, and a small amount of tobacco. But more than anything I would like to make a trade with young William."

Somewhat startled, Zeke and William looked at each other, Zeke asked, "what would thet be, Frenchy, thet boy ain't got anythang a'tall?"

Jean-Pierre gave his most pleasant trading face and stated, "I

---

59   Musket referred to long firearms which had no riflings, spiral grooves within the barrel to hold the bullet straight in flight. They typically were large bore, about .60 to .75 caliber, and could be used for bird shot as well as round ball. They were heavy in weight with only short range capability, but typically more reliable than rifles. The word musket always referred to a military long firearm, never one designed for civilian use. During the American Civil War, "rifled muskets" were manufactured to gain greater accuracy.

was hoping that I could persuade young William to use his great skill to shape a pirogue for me that I might use on my journey down the great Riviere Blanche."

Somewhat taken aback, the two Talbot men sat silently and thought out the proposition. It confused them that someone would want to trade for something that at this time did not exist. Neither of the men ever gave thought to working for remuneration.

"I would give young William eight beaver peltries for his time and skill, and two more for the use of his own small pirogue for a short trip up the Riviere Blanche," offered Jean-Pierre.

William looked to his father who started to speak, then stopped to think again. He raised his right hand to scratch his bearded chin. After a long pause, he said that he reckoned that should be a fair trade, as he considered that William was getting ten beaver peltries for basically nothing.

"Tres bien, Monsieur," exclaimed Jean-Pierre, "we have an agreement then. I shall leave now to travel up the Riviere Blanche into the mountains for the few days it shall require young William to fashion my own pirogue. It is too wonderful an opportunity to miss as I am so close. I have been much disappointed in coming down the Riviere Noire without the use of a pirogue to explore the riviers of the western mountains."

After giving William a few instructions regarding the size and style of the watercraft, Jean-Pierre dropped his few possessions into the small pirogue and slipped it out into the current. Pointing the bow of the small craft into the oncoming current, Jean-Pierre dug the paddle deep into the river's surface, forcing it upstream. Waving a goodbye to the Talbots assembled on the river bank, Jean-Pierre shouted joyfully, "Merci, mes amis, I shall return in one week's time to exchange the pirogues." With this farewell, he paddled the small craft up the Riviere Blanche.

His blood flowed strong this day as he again was paddling up a fresh mountain river. The nature of the voyageur was deep within him, as he preferred travel by pirogue to any other, particularly more so than walking overland. Hour after hour he held a fast pace, his well-trained muscles working the paddle and craft easily.

As Jean-Pierre passed through the high land between the bottoms and the mountains, he passed a well-worn trail that crossed the river from southwest to northeast. He had heard of it from other French traders, and the Talbots had mentioned it as well. It was called the Great Southwest Trail, used for centuries by Indians and now by white men who journeyed between Saint Louis and Petit Rocher.[60]

---

60 The Great Southwest Trail extended from the present area of St. Louis, Missouri (old Cahokia, an Indian village, east of the Mississippi River, of an earlier time) southwest diagonally across the present state of Arkansas, crossing the Red River near the present location of Texarkana, Arkansas. In this vicinity, it became known as the Chihuahua Trail. It probably extended on to that Mexican region. Long distance trails such as the Great Southwest Trail were common across North America as the Indian peoples had need of long distance travel for trade and war. Typically, they followed high land. The Great Southwest Trail followed the eastern edge of the Ozark Mountains, allowing travelers to escape the toilsome journey up and over high mountain ridges or through flooded bottomland. There was possibly no one exact trail in most locales, but rather a general direction of travel. Petit Rocher (pronounced puh-tee ro-shay) was the French name for Little Rock, Arkansas. It was so named for the location of a noticeable rock on the south bank of the Arkansas River. A much larger rock was noted farther up the river. Both these served as markers for French traders over many year, being called "little rock" and "big rock." The location of the smaller rock was of more importance as it was at the crossing of the Great Southwest Trail. Also, for American settlers coming up the Arkansas River, this was the first high land providing protection from yearly flooding and the threat of malaria.

Nightfall found him entering the mountains, so he sought a campsite for the night, choosing a gravelly bar near where a bayou flowed from the north.[61] From several old campsites that were visible in the area, it was evident many other river travelers had stopped here. He noted a deadfall on one end of the bar and heeding an old instinct, chose a spot nearby for his camp. Here he would have all the wood he needed for his cook fire. In addition to the deadfall being his ready source of firewood, it would also keep anyone from coming down the bar from that side without making a great deal of noise while coming through the dry wood. His senses also valued the overhanging bank above the sand bar, which was taller than a man. The bank would reflect heat from the fire while keeping him from being seen from the land side. He also noted with satisfaction that the large tree immediately above the camp site was a sycamore. The surface of the ground below it would be covered with large dry leaves, making it impossible for anyone to approach his camp silently from that side. Such things always had to be considered by someone who traveled alone in the wilderness.

The Talbots had sternly warned him against going very far upstream for he would risk running into a band of roving Osage who they said were never friendly. Jean-Pierre did not have to be told of the nature of the Osage, but doubted that they would be this far from their winter quarters. He knew that their main village was far to the northwest, near the Riviere Missouri. But, of course, in this wilderness there were others who would strike down a traveler

---

61   Poke Bayou is believed to have been settled about 1817, though possibly before that date. This is the general area where our fictional character camped that night. It is now the site of Batesville, Arkansas, one of the oldest settlements in Arkansas. Poke Bayou is a stream which flows south into the White River at Batesville.

if given the opportunity. His survival instincts told him always to have his lance with arms reach.

Satisfied with his choice of a site, Jean-Pierre set about making his camp. After taking some dry grass from his fire making kit, he took out his flint, striker and char cloth. A shower of sparks was sent from the flint into the char cloth. Slow, even breaths brightened them into an intense heat. This then was set under the dry grass. Within seconds, Jean-Pierre had the beginnings of his cook fire. While this was building, he gathered more wood from the deadfall. Later he took his bag of foodstuffs from the pirogue and began to fashion a supper of cornpone and broiled fish. Madame Talbot had been generous in giving him some corn meal for his trip up the Riviere Blanche. On the trip upriver, Jean-Pierre had kept a baited line in the water behind the pirogue, catching two perch and a bass for his supper.

Jean-Pierre put his supper together. He used his tea cup to mix the corn meal with warm water and salt, then worked it by hand into a round, flat cake. Earlier,a smooth rock had been picked from the bar and placed in the fire to heat. Now this rock was pulled with a stick to the fire's edge. The small corn meal cakes were placed upon the hot stone to bake. The fish were dressed and stuck through with green limbs before being set above the hot coals to broil.

Lying upon a spot of smooth sand, Jean-Pierre watched his supper cook as he listened to the night sounds of this great mountain river. Occasionally he heard the calls of the night birds. On this night he reflected upon his younger years, possibly because of having seen the Talbot children. There were missed opportunities through the years, like having a wife for companionship. He, himself, could have as many children as Zeke Talbot. But then he wondered if he could have remained in one location as was needed to bring up a family. Maybe his traveling nature was why he never took a wife. But even without the wife and children, he had enjoyed his years. Truly, he was a fortunate man, even if he had missed the opportunity of traveling to the far ocean with the Captains Lewis and Clark.

For two days Jean-Pierre Paddled the pirogue upstream, always marveling at the beauty of the white stone bluffs which frequently rose high above the river. More than once he said to himself that truly this was a beautiful land. He also noted that the farther he traveled, the clearer the river water became until he could often see the bottom clearly at depths of many feet. Its nature was a succession of shallow rapids over shelves of rock, followed by long stretches of deep green pools.

At one point, a small bayou came into the Riviere Blanche from the north. Curious as to its promise of furs, Jean-Pierre paddled his way upstream until the signs of beaver began to appear. Here he set his trapline, camping under one of the high outcroppings of limestone which were common in these mountains.

He stayed on this small bayou for three days, taking several furs of beaver and raccoon, but only one mink. During the days he walked the valleys and ridges in the immediate vicinity, entertaining himself with this new landscape of high ridges, steep limestone bluffs, and clear running bayous.

All too soon he was forced to return down the Riviere Blanche. Time would not now allow any further exploration of this beautiful mountain river. Jean-Pierre kept the small pirogue to a fast pace as he was anxious to exchange it for the larger one young William was making for him. But he deeply regretted having to leave these mountains and their lovely Riviere Blanche after only a taste of what they held. Perhaps another winter he could return for several months to explore and trap. Now he needed to make his way on down the Riviere Blanche. The Talbots had told him that the spring rains would be flooding the bottomlands, making it next to impossible to work traps.

Late that afternoon he arrived at the Talbot clearing as the trip down had taken little time with the fast current. When he landed, he found William working over a new pirogue on the river bank, surprised and seemingly pleased to see Jean-Pierre. "Mister Vilernew, I've got it all ready fer ya, how ya like it?" asked Williams with great pride?

Quickly stepping from the smaller craft, Jean-Pierre spoke excitedly, "Tres bien, Monsieur William, it is quite better than I had even hoped. It shall take Jean-Pierre far and fast as you American say." Jean-Pierre was genuinely pleased with the pirogue. It had beautiful form, well rounded inside and not a single flat spot or splinter showed. It was almost fifteen feet long, one and one half feet in depth, and just over two feet in width. It was bright in the sunshine with the yellowish look of fresh cypress.

Together they examined and talked of the craft's light weight, handling capabilities and weight capacity, both sharing each other's enthusiasm in this work of wood. Below the craft lay a thick pile of chips and shavings which had been taken from the log to shape the pirogue. When the younger children later joined the two men at the river bank, William directed them to fetch a basket and haul these wood chips to the cabin where they would be used for starting fires. In the backwoods, few things were wasted.

The family was glad to see him, making Jean-Pierre feel good within himself. A man without a family of his own had to take affection where he found it. And this backwoods Hoosier family could for a short space of time fill one of the emotional voids in his life.

As on their first evening together, the Talbots and their guest sat late into the night, sharing tobacco, the jug of whiskey and countless stories of the frontier. In a sense the Talbots were as alone as Jean-Pierre, living here over one hundred miles from the nearest trading post. There were other families such as theirs, but they were separated by many miles of roadless wilderness. The mountains were steep and heavily wooded, while the bottomland was a succession of cane brakes, sloughs, backwater, fallen logs, and heavy timber. The only travel with any ease at all was by water, but that was difficult if a family was moving up against the current with a heavy load of possessions.

At dawn the next morning Jean-Pierre paddled his new pirogue through the juncture of the Noire and the Blanche, proceeding south down the latter. Shortly after the juncture, he eased the pirogue into a protective shield of a brushy point and tied off the new watercraft. It was time to retrieve the furs and other items from his cache. Jean-Pierre made the short walk from the river to the hollow log chosen for its obscurity. Everything was just as he had left it. He had been confident that his cache would remain unnoticed should anyone happen to walk through the area. Of course, the primary security factor was that these bottoms were seldom traveled by anyone, white or Indian.

With his cache carried back to the pirogue, Jean-Pierre moved on downstream to the old river channel where the raft had been secreted. This, too, was in place. He felt fortunate as river pirates always seemed to be about working their own trade. He resolved to be especially careful in the days ahead as he traveled downriver. It was quite possible that he might encounter one of these roving bands of murderers and thieves.

Chapter Five

Down the Riviere Blanche

After retrieving his cache of furs and poling the raft with the pirogue in tow, Jean-Pierre waited until nightfall before pushing out into the current of the White. He still had no firearm and was alone in a day when thieves went virtually unchecked. His winter's catch of furs would be a big prize for river pirates, and at this time of the year they would be laying in wait for such trappers as himself. Under cover of darkness he began the next stage of his journey, down the Riviere Blanche to the Mississippi. Near midnight he passed what the Talbots had called Hackington's Station. This had long been a crossing for the Chickasaws on fall hunting trips into the western mountains, and some white men had settled there. Now it was supposed to be abandoned.

Travel was slow going down the Riviere Blanche as the raft would go no faster than the speed of the current. Jean-Pierre was tempted to abandon it for the much faster pirogue. But he knew that the raft, though slow, was a better option. On the raft he could cook and sleep comfortably without finding dry land. During the trip, he could trap only where there was high land not yet covered by flood waters. Soon after the beginning of his journey all of the land was flooded. Water completely surrounded the timber in all directions. But after several days, he found higher ground to the west of the river. Here he found good trapping and stayed a few days. This late in the season, he could not pass up any opportunities of taking furs.

The farther south he traveled, the more flooding he encountered. When he did find high ground, the trapping was good as many fur bearing animals had taken refuge from the spring floods. Jean-Pierre stopped for several days whenever he found opportunities for trapping. And whenever a bayou entered the Riviere Blanche, he tied off the raft and explored the smaller waterway with the pirogue. These forays gained him many more furs than if he had been forced to stay with the main river. But as he floated farther south, high land became almost impossible to find. By this time, though, he had a large cache of furs. This was in spite of the interruption of his winter's plans by the earthquakes. From time to time he passed a small settlement. At most of these he merely gestured a greeting and drifted on, not wanting to invite the theft of his furs if they learned that he had no firearm.

Many of his days were spent continually drifting downstream, an activity which grew somewhat monotonous. The frequent passing of ducks overhead was a welcome diversion. It seemed to Jean-Pierre that the farther he floated, the slower the raft moved. The almost daily rains often kept him wet and cold. Fortunately, the weather was warming with each day; otherwise, he would have constantly been chilled. Because of all the flooding, it was difficult to find dry wood for his fire.

With trapping impossible much of the time, the only thing he had to do was watch the scenery. Jean-Pierre never tired of looking at the trees and the wildlife which lived in and around them. His only work responsibility now was to keep his attention was guiding the raft past the ever-present driftwood. The level of the river had risen so high that the water must have stretched for miles beyond the river's banks. The high water allowed the current to flow as much overland as within the main channel. Of course, the raft could not be navigated through the woods.

It required diligence to keep the raft contained within the channel. Fortunately, Jean-Pierre had no difficulty in knowing the location of the channel as it was quite wide and bordered by definite lines of heavy timber. After some days of the high water, he resigned himself to not being able to do any more trapping this spring. From what he had heard about the terrain to the south, he imagined that, with the exception of the high ridge somewhere to the east, the flooded woods spread all the way to the Fleuve Mississippi.

He was now passing through deep bottom country. The heavily timbered bottoms stretched for many miles in every direction. These were bounded on the east by the ridge which he had crossed after leaving the Grand Marais and on the west by the mountains. From Jean-Pierre's few opportunities to explore away from the river, he knew the landscape to be crisscrossed by fallen trees and sloughs, as well as great thickets of briars or cane. He wondered how anyone could possibly cross it overland with any more than what they could carry on their back. Certainly, it was an insurmountable obstacle to wagons.[62]

---

62 Whereas the prairie schooner enabled the later American settlers to traverse the Great Plains easily, much of the southern woodlands was initially impenetrable by wagon. Thick timber, cane and briars along with innumerable river channels, sloughs and boggy soil from frequent flooding presented a formidable obstacle for the wagon traveler. This was the terrain of eastern Arkansas. The rivers were the highways of settlement and commerce until about 1830 when the federal government began building roads for military purposes. One such road followed the direction of the Great Southwest Trail, now U.S. highway 67 from St. Louis through Little Rock. Another was a road from Memphis to Little Rock.

He knew that silt had been deposited here by floods like the present one for thousands of years. With the rich alluvial soil and an ample supply of water, the land produced great trees which seemed to reach the sky above. They grew tall and straight, competing for the sunlight. There were oak, gum, elm, pecan, ash, hickory, and many other species along the high ridges. Cypress and water tupelo grew principally along the waterways. Throughout the bottoms, it was common to see cypress and oak four feet in diameter. Some were much larger.[63] Giant cypress sentinels lined the river's edge, holding high aloft gnarled branches aged over centuries. Runways of worn bark showed that many small animals made their homes in the hollows of these castles in the sky.

There was an abundance of undergrowth along the river channel where sunlight was more available. Small trees, bushes, and briars could at times block visibility. From the river channel, the woods often appeared impenetrable. This would become much more pronounced with summer foliage. And there was no view of the horizon as the tall timber obscured everything except the river channel.

Late one afternoon, Jean-Pierre's attention on the raft was interrupted by a darkness which seemed to be closing over the river. There was also a growing dampness in the air. Thinking that this was only another rain front coming from the west, Jean-Pierre set about securing his furs and foodstuffs under the canvas.

---

63   In the early 1960's, the author's father cut a cypress on their farm in Greene County, Arkansas, that was almost seven feet in diameter. It should also be noted that this tree had grown beside the natural Cache River where the accumulation of silt over the centuries had buried its original base. The stump had 583 growth rings. It had been over one hundred years old when Columbus discovered America and one hundred and fifty years old when Hernando de Soto crossed into Arkansas.

Jean-Pierre paid little heed when light rain began to fall. He had been rained on so many times during his life that he gave light rain little notice. Then the heavy rumbling of thunder came to him from the west. On down the river he guided the raft, intent on shortening the distance to the great Mississippi. He knew the front was getting closer when long lightning bolts flashed overhead. Ripping through the dark sky, their brilliance was followed by loud echoing booms of thunder. Despite the weather warnings, he continued to follow the current down river, hoping to escape the brunt of the storm.

Suddenly, the sound of heavy rain came from the west and the traveler began to become concerned. Jean-Pierre knew that if he were caught out on the river in a driving rainstorm, his vision might be obscured to the extent that he could lose control of the raft. A wreck in which he lost both furs and raft would be disastrous. He decided to tie up at the west bank under some shelter and wait out the heavier part of the storm. He guided the raft into a stand of large cypress along the west bank and made use of the shelter of their bulk.

Jean-Pierre sat in his canvas shelter and prepared to watch the storm front blow past. He thought that in a few minutes this spring storm would pass and he could continue on his way with little inconvenience. Soon hard rain came, then rain so hard that he could not see the eastern bank. At times the wall of white around him would shift as the winds picked up, blowing the heavy rain about like dust. The canvas sagged under the weight of the water and wind until the frame suspending it collapsed. Still he sat there, with only his face sticking out from the sodden canvas. He knew that there was nothing else he could do and nowhere else he could go.

After what seemed like an eternity of heavy rain and high winds, another sound came to him. There was some sort of roar rising in the west. Suddenly the wind increased even more, blowing large pieces of wooden debris through the air like so many dry leaves. These clattered through the limbs of the trees as they bounced off the timber. The wind became so high that the heavily soaked canvas would have blown off him if he had not held tightly onto it.

When he didn't think the storm could get any worse, the roaring sound became so loud that he was sure that he could not even have heard his own scream. The river was a turmoil of whipping water and debris. Both rain and hail fell in torrents as if the sky had ripped open. He gritted his teeth as the hailstones pounded him through the sodden canvas. Huddled there, he hung on for his life, hoping that his woven rope of hickory bark would hold the raft secure under the pressure of the wind and the current. He realized that the raft, if torn loose by the current and slammed hard against something solid, could break up, dropping himself and his winter's furs into the river. Surely, even a strong swimmer could drown out in the frothy river. The thought came to him that if one did not drown in the river itself, he could surely drown in the deluge of water from above.

Then an explosion of sound and movement came from just downriver. The deafening roar seemed to erupt as if it had exploded out of itself. Jean-Pierre stared as the large trees along the river exploded or were stripped of their limbs. Now in addition to the downpour of rain, came a torrent of wooden debris, dangerously flying in all directions.

In the dim light of the storm, he saw a great beast approach the river at a curve in the channel, just one hundred yards below him. It was dark and tall, standing much higher than the trees, and it ripped apart everything in its path. Again, and again, Jean-Pierre cried aloud, "Mon Dieu, Mon Dieu." But he could only hear his words in his own mind as the roar of the beast was too great.

It started across the river but fell back as if repelled by the river's strength. It tore tall trees from their roots and hurled them into the river. With an even greater roar it again started across the river, but again it was forced back after a short distance. It fell back farther into the timber. For an instant Jean-Pierre felt relief, believing that the beast had quit the area. Still there was heavy rain and high winds. The roar seemed to have lessened.

Just then it came again with more fervor than before. Jean-Pierre could see the dark shape of the beast approaching the river at great speed. With tremendous destruction, it again tore its way through the timber, tearing whole trees from the ground in its wake. The frightened traveler on the small raft sat paralyzed with fear, unable even to cry out, and with no one to hear him if he did.

This time, the beast hurled itself across the width of the river at a level higher above the water, sucking huge volumes of water up into itself as it passed. Jean-Pierre could see this clearly. It was almost as if the water from the river was falling upward. When the dark beast struck the timber of the eastern bank, another great explosion occurred. Every fabric of the trees in its path seemed to explode into the air. All the water which had been sucked up into its center now was forced outward in all directions, causing waves upon the river. Missiles rained upon the traveler on the raft across the river, some of them with enough force to bring sharp pain. Twice, limbs as large as a man's leg struck the raft. The craft seemed flimsy as it bobbed wildly on the river.

Finally, the beast passed on through the timber to the east, leaving a wide path of destruction in its wake. Now in its absence, stillness lay heavy on the solitary traveler. Sitting there on the Riviere Blanche, utterly drenched, sorely bruised and so frightened that he could not even stand, Jean-Pierre almost wished that the great earthquake had swallowed him. Then he would have been saved from this terrible ordeal.

After a time, he crawled slowly out from the wet canvas and began to assess the damage. Four of the cypress floor poles had been shattered. The ties of hickory bark were unraveling in almost every joint. All his furs lay in a sodden heap. His few stores of food appeared to be in the same condition. But he was greatly relieved when he found his new pirogue to be undamaged.

Silently, Jean-Pierre looked about him. Everything in sight appeared broken, splintered, or uprooted. The devastated wilderness was soaked and dripping from the torrential downpour. Except for the sounds of dripping water, the river scene was silent. All the land creatures had either escaped out of the storm's path or had been killed in its wake. He had on many occasions heard from others about their experiences with tornadoes, but this had been his first. Jean-Pierre untied the damaged raft and guided it downstream to an open space on the riverbank. Stepping off onto the hail-covered ground, he fell to his knees, looked skyward and touched out the shape of the cross upon his chest. He gave thanks to God for once again saving his life when it was all but lost. Looking back through the timber from which the storm had come, he saw a wide strip of desolation, as if a cannon ball as large as a hill had been shot through the trees. He knew that he was truly fortunate to be alive.

Surely, the greatness of God must have been greater than that of the storm.

Once he regained his composure, he set about making a camp. Before darkness set in he wanted a roaring fire with which he could dry out his furs and camp articles. As all the wood was drenched from the storm, he had to chop open a decaying log to find enough dry wood to start his fire. With only a sparse meal that evening of dried fish, Jean-Pierre kept busy building drying racks from scraps of debris. Over these, he draped the furs and the canvas to dry.

Early the next morning, he began repairing the raft before continuing downriver. With the axe he cut out the large limbs which had punctured the floor poles. Then, new cypress poles were cut from the riverbank as replacements. Also, fresh hickory bark was gathered and all the raft joints repaired.

With his furs dried and the raft repaired, Jean-Pierre shoved off from the destruction of the storm. He was anxious to distance himself from the place as the memory of his near-death experience was still very fresh.

Two days after his brush with the tornado, Jean-Pierre began to suffer from a lack of food. He had been unable to catch enough fish since the storm. As the river had again shifted away from the higher ground to the west, he had not had an opportunity to take any game.

Fortune seemed to smile when he saw a squirrel farther downriver. If it had been in a tree, there would have been little chance of killing it, but this squirrel was swimming across the river. Quickly, he untied the pirogue and set out to intercept it before it reached the safety of the other side.

With great force, he drove the paddle deep into the river.

The pirogue responded by slicing through the river's surface. The distance shortened quickly. In these few seconds, the woodsman formed a plan. His need was to first catch the squirrel and then to kill it. If he had brought the bow to shoot it, it could have sunk before he could retrieve it. And, if he struck it with the paddle, the blow itself could drive it below the surface and away from his grasp. If he used the paddle to bring it into the pirogue alive, the agile creature would as quickly escape back to the river.

As the squirrel neared the bank, a plan came to him. With all speed, he drove the craft forward in its approach. With only a few feet between them, the woodsman set his plan in motion. He would drive the pirogue to pass directly in front of the squirrel, forcing it to swim alongside until he could grasp its tail. With one swift motion, he would jerk the squirrel from the water, swing it up and then sharply down, bringing its head down against the bottom of the pirogue. He believed that this would surely work without giving the squirrel any opportunity to claw or bite his hand.

With only a few feet of river to spare, the front of the pirogue cut off the squirrel's escape. As the woodsman had planned, the creature tried to swim around the front of the pirogue. As the distance shortened, he reached out his right hand in readiness of taking hold of the long tail. For an instant, only inches separated his hand from the squirrel's tail. Already, he could taste the meal.

But suddenly there came a great splash from the depths of the river. In an instant, a large shape raised itself from the depths of the river to engulf the squirrel. Water rose in its wake and splashed all over Jean-Pierre and the pirogue. Such was the force of the wake that the pirogue itself was almost upset. Jean-Pierre had to grasp the sides with both hands to steady it. Looking down at the river's surface, he saw no squirrel. It was gone. Instead of becoming his meal, it had now become the meal of some giant fish.

Shaken, he sat still a moment to collect his thoughts about what had just happened. This fish was the largest Jean-Pierre had ever seen. He remembered it clearly from the instant it had appeared at the surface. Its mouth was long and pointed, projecting out beyond its body. And the width of the fish seemed to have been at least a foot. As the fish's body had risen and passed along the surface before it reentered the depths, it appeared to have been as long as Jean-Pierre was tall.[64]

For a moment, he looked at his right hand, wondering what would have happened if he had caught hold of the squirrel's tail an instant sooner. He believed such a fish might have taken his hand with the squirrel. Looking from the river's surface to the sky above, Jean-Pierre spoke aloud some words of thanks, "Merci beaucoup, Mon Dieu."

He now recovered the raft and thought much less of his hunger. That afternoon he passed by the mouth of a small river which emptied into the Riviere Blanche from the north. Though he could not be sure, he speculated that this could be the Riviere Cache. Here the fish began to bite once again, so the woodsman had food to sustain himself.

---

64 The Alligator Gar is native to Arkansas waters, in particular, the White and St. Francis rivers. It commonly grows to six feet in length, weighing over sixty pounds, and one had weighed at 120 pounds. The species is considered to be prehistoric in origin.

CHAPTER SIX

Poste aux Arkansas

SEVERAL WEEKS AFTER JEAN-PIERRE HAD LEFT the Riviere Noire, he passed a large channel flowing in from the right bank. Curious about the new source of water, he tied the raft off securely so that he might take the pirogue and investigate this waterway. He knew there was something about the channel that he should remember. After countless fireside stories from other trappers and traders, it was impossible to remember them all. But he prided himself on having maps inside his head, not only of places where he had traveled, but even of those he had only heard about around a campfire. About a week prior, he had observed a smaller river entering the Riviere Blanche from the west. This he had deduced was the Petite Riviere Rouge.[65]

He worked the pirogue against the current, sorting out the channel between the giant trees of the deep woods. He was curious about this channel and decided to go upstream to learn more of it. He had traveled less than a league when suddenly before him a great river passed. Pulling up beside a small cypress, Jean-Pierre held the craft steady with one hand on a low-hanging limb. It was a long way to the timber on the other side. It was then that an old

---

65   Petit Riviere Rouge translates from the French into Little Red River. It flows out of the Ozark Mountains and enters the White River east of Searcy, Arkansas. The Little Red fills Greer's Ferry Lake.

story came back to him. This great waterway before him was none other than the Riviere Arkansas, which was said to take its origin in the great mountains of the far west. Awed by the discovery and realization, Jean-Pierre sat there for several minutes, watching the strong current of the great river flow on down to the Mississippi.[66]

Having enjoyed his moment of discovery, Jean-Pierre turned his pirogue back toward the raft. He realized that if he had stayed longer with the Talbots, he would have learned more about the rivers. However, the inconvenience had added some adventure and mystery to a succession of monotonous days. By the time he reached the raft, a plan had formed in his mind. Instead of paddling a loaded pirogue up the Fleuve Mississippi and trading his furs at St. Louis, he would go the short distance up the Riviere Arkansas and trade them at Poste aux Arkansas.[67] His sense of adventure would not allow him to leave this region without having had his pirogue upon the Arkansas.

Returning to the Blanche, Jean-Pierre moved the raft to a secluded location. As was common along the river, a heavy strip of briars and brush lined the main channel. It was behind one of these

---

66   The White River Cut-off was an act of nature that was used extensively by keelboatmen. It would cut fifty miles off the distance traveled between the middle Mississippi Valley and the Arkansas Valley. Today, the old cut-off is closed off, but a man-made channel exists for the same purpose, complete with a lock system. The Arkansas River has its origins in the Rocky Mountains.

67   Arkansas Post is one of the oldest white settlements west of the Mississippi River. It is located about sixty miles up the Arkansas from the Mississippi River. It was settled in 1686 by Henri de Tonty, and associate of the French explorer La Salle. From its beginnings, it served both as a military and trading outpost for the French, Spanish and American. Its lowland location prevented it from becoming a large center and necessitated relocation on several occasions. It served as the first territorial capital of Arkansas from 1819 until 1821.

that he guided the raft toward and secured it to several small trees. Now it could settle to the ground should it remain here when the flood waters receded. In the meantime, it was out of sight of river pirates. There was still some chance that he might need the raft. In the wilderness, any cache of resources could in the future mean the difference between life and death.

With the raft secured, Jean-Pierre loaded everything of value into the pirogue and pointed it back up the overflow channel. From what he had been told, Poste aux Arkansas was located upstream about twenty leagues from the Mississippi, but he did not know how far it was from this channel to the Poste. As it was now about mid-afternoon, he doubted that he could reach the Poste before dark but was too excited to remain with the raft until the next morning.

Setting out in the pirogue heavily laden with furs, his travel up the overflow channel was much slower on this trip. And upon entering the strong flood current of the Arkansas, he found the going even more difficult. The great river at flood stage carried a tremendous volume of water with a fast current. At this point solid ground was not visible anywhere. Only a line of tall timber marked the course of the main channel. On more than one occasion he had to work to miss a drifting tree.

At nightfall, he still had not reached the Poste and was concerned that he would miss it altogether in the darkness. But now another dilemma presented itself. There was not a piece of high land showing above the flood waters. This was a situation when the raft would be appreciated as he had been able to sleep comfortably and cook his meals while on the raft. However, it would have been impossible to move the raft upstream against the current.

The veteran woodsman felt somewhat powerless against the

flood waters of the great river. The force of the muddy current was awesome. Dangerous currents threatened to drive him into the many drifting trees. The onset of darkness compounded his concern. Continuing to paddle upstream, Jean-Pierre considered his options, which were not many. He could, of course, work his way through the timber and away from the main channel in hopes of reaching dry land. Though eventually he would, he well knew that high land could be miles from the channel, possibly as far as the east side of the Riviere Blanche.

Or, he could go on upriver hoping that the Poste would have a lantern out for travelers such as himself. But, if he passed it and morning came without having seen it, he would not know for certain whether it lay above or below him on the river. There was only one other option that he could see, and he believed that he should take it quickly before full darkness overtook him. Paddling now with all his strength, Jean-Pierre looked for an opening in the timber away from the stronger current. Finding one, he paddled into a cluster of timber. He used a strong rawhide rope to tie the stern of the craft off short to a willow oak about four feet in diameter. Thus secured, the pirogue naturally stayed in the protected hollow formed where the huge tree split the current.

Rearranging his bales of furs, he fashioned a bed for his long frame. After several hours at the paddle, this would be a welcome relief. Leaning his shoulders against the stern, he sought rest after the afternoon's work. As much as he enjoyed paddling a pirogue, he was unaccustomed to the work after his long overland journey. The short trip up the Blanche from the Talbot's cabin was too short and too long ago to strengthen him sufficiently for the hard work here on the Arkansas at flood stage.

He watched the flood waters pass by in the fading light as he ate a supper of dried fish, with only river water to wash it down. He realized that if he had stayed with the raft until morning, he would have had a fire and something hot to drink tonight. To Jean-Pierre, the excitement of being closer to Poste aux Arkansas offset that completely. Besides, a lifetime of wilderness travels had accustomed him to what town folks would call extreme hardship. In the early evening, he settled into the pile of furs and let the soft gurgling sound of the current lull him into a deep sleep.

Dawn found Jean-Pierre slowly working his way against the flood stage current of the Riviere Arkansas. With only dried fish and flood water for his breakfast, there was nothing else to do but to paddle on upriver where he might find a better camp. Sleeping in the pirogue had left his muscles cramped, and there had been nowhere to walk them out and no fire to heat water to warm his insides. Fortunately, the weather was warm with no indication of rain.

After about two hours he caught sight of man-made markings on some trees on the north side of the river. He knew these to be French signs of a settlement nearby. Without hesitation, he turned the pirogue toward them, working his way carefully through the flooded timber. After a time of following this marked trail, he saw several pirogues tied at a makeshift landing. He joined them and walked up what was by now a well-worn trail. Here he could see a clearing with several structures. There were several houses and outbuildings, all of a French character. All the structures were raised off the ground. The houses had galleries around the exteriors and hip roofs.

"Ah, mais mon Dieu, ce sont des Francais," quickly he stepped toward the nearer house of this small French village.[68]

As Jean-Pierre approached, a French-Canadian hailed him from one of the doorways. "Bonjour, mon ami, welcome to our village."

It lifted Jean-Pierre's spirits greatly to hear words spoken in his own tongue. Stepping briskly now toward the approaching villager, Jean-Pierre called out, "Je m'appelle Jean-Pierre Villeneuve, de Ste. Genevieve sur le Fleuve Mississippi."

"Et je suis Claude Hebert. Welcome, Jean-Pierre Villeneuve to our village on the Riviere Arkansas. Have you been trapping the furs?" noting the cargo in Jean-Pierre's pirogue.

"Oui, monsieur Hebert. I have been gone all the fall and winter taking furs upon the Riviere St. Francois and the Riviere Noire as well as the Riviere Blanche," responded Jean-Pierre.

Speaking now in shock, Claude Hebert asked, "Were you caught up in the shaking of the earth then?"

"Oui, that I was. And only the hand of God saved me from being swallowed up into the bowels of the earth. But I survived and am now traveling to Poste aux Arkansas to trade some of my furs."

"It is but a short distance up the river. But first you must come into our village to rest and share your travels with us," stated Claude Hebert. "It is so infrequent that another Frenchman comes our way since the Americans have taken over Louisiane. We shall celebrate, Oui?"[69]

---

68 Though this story is fiction, there were two French houses in this area at the time, very close to the actual site of the first post. The Menard family, long time residents of the area, occupied one house. This was the first high ground upstream from the Mississippi River, a welcome refuge during high water.

69 While Americans on the frontier preferred to live in dwellings

With that exchange, the two walked into the village. Though there were only a few houses, Jean-Pierre was gratified to sense the structure of French society once again around him. Claude Hebert introduced Jean-Pierre to everyone present and asked his own wife, Monique, to make them coffee and begin a festive meal for the evening.

Jean-Pierre stayed two nights with these newly made friends. Everyone enjoyed the occasion of fresh French companionship. There was talk of many things, particularly of things along the rivers. They talked of the changes in their French culture in the few years since the Americans had taken control of Louisiane. They all agreed that life under the Spanish had not been so bad. Except for a few soldiers and government officials, the Spanish government had never endeavored to settle their own people in Louisiane. The Spanish had allowed the French to continue their village life as it had been for almost a hundred years before.[70] Unlike the Spanish,

---

on their own farms, the French chose to live in villages. Streets were typically small and twisted and often littered with farm equipment where a jovial Frenchman had left it. Shops were in the front of homes instead of in separate quarters. The farmers went out to a common field to work their crops and to a common pasture to graze their livestock. The use of common fields occurred in England as well as France. Common fields were known to have been used in southeast Missouri, but not in Arkansas. Socialization with others was much more a part of a Frenchman's life than with Americans.

70 The Spanish gained what is known as the Louisiana Purchase from the French in 1762 and returned it to them in 1800. During this time the Spanish made little or no effort to build villages or populate the area with their own people. Part of their motivation for accepting Louisiana was to provide a buffer between the Americans and their more valuable holdings in Texas. A government and military presence was maintained by Spanish authorities. The French culture which was prevalent throughout the region was uninterrupted.

the American government was encouraging its people to migrate westward and settle the new lands. This influx of Americans was beginning to change the lives of the French. Many Frenchmen had moved west across the Fleuve Mississippi after the American colonies acquired control of the Illinois and Kentucky area, but now there was nowhere close for the French to relocate. Also, they speculated about the possibility of a war between the American colonies and the British, as tensions had been rising for several years. Certainly, none of these Frenchmen had any love for the British.[71]

The great quake had shaken them here, and most of the daily aftershocks were still being felt, but there had been no real damage beyond a few trees falling and an occasional utensil falling from its hook on a wall. Nonetheless, it was a subject which caused much concern among these isolated French villagers. And, of course, Frenchmen never got together without the subject of furs being discussed at great length.

On the morning of his departure from the French settlement, Jean-Pierre was relieved that the flood waters had receded somewhat, giving more definition to the main river channel. The two nights with fellow Frenchmen had boosted his spirits and he paddled the remaining miles in a cheerful frame of mind. They had eaten, drank and spoken French, all quite a delight for Jean-Pierre. And now he wore a new shirt, brightly embroidered by Madame Hebert and given to him as a parting gift in return for the merriment he had brought to them.

In the late afternoon, he saw a settlement along a red bluff on

---

71 The French and English had fought over control of certain parts of North America for over one hundred years. At this time, the Napoleonic wars were being fought in Europe. Anger was deeply rooted on both sides.

the north bank which he thought must be Poste aux Arkansas. It did not appear to be an imposing settlement, much less than Jean-Pierre had anticipated. All of his life he had heard stories about this place, though his travels had never brought him this far south.[72]

Choosing an empty spot at the landing, Jean-Pierre drove his pirogue upon the bank among the odd assortment of other water crafts. There were pirogues of varying sizes, one birch bark canoe, two rafts larger than his own, and three keelboats. After securing his own pirogue to one of the many large stakes driven into the soil for this purpose, he stood briefly to stretch his muscles. As he did so, he surveyed the poste. There were a good many buildings, though not really a village like Ste. Genevieve. He estimated that there were less than five hundred living in the entire village, with about fifty structures loosely spread over the surrounding area. The buildings were elevated off the ground to protect the inhabitants from flooding. Galleries surrounded the houses, typically on all sides, and tall chimneys rose above the roofs. In the style of the French, exposed timbers framed the roof. He reasoned that this was to be expected as the poste had been French for over one hundred years. The Americans had been in possession of it less than ten.

Now he made his way toward what looked like a trading house. Casks of varying sizes were stacked out in front while bales of furs filled a large lean-to on the side of the building. On that side of the house was the fur press used for compacting bales of

---

72 At the time Arkansas Post consisted of about forty to fifty houses in the immediate area, with about fifteen of those in the village itself. There were probably about four hundred to five hundred people in residence. Over the one hundred and seventeen years of French and Spanish control, the post was moved several times. In 1779, it was relocated to Ecor Rouge (red bluff), its present location.

furs for shipment down to Nouvelle Orleans. Several men loitered about the place, some turning to look intently at Jean-Pierre. At a glance, any of them could tell that he was a French-Indian trapper. His heritage was evident both from his facial features and his dress. This was obvious to anyone familiar with the people of the middle Mississippi Valley.

Jean-Pierre, in turn, looked over the lot of them. Some of them were French like himself, as with him this was obvious from their dress. The colorful shirts were quick indicators of their French culture. He assumed those who were not French were probably Americans, but as Poste aux Arkansas was a crossroads for travelers from all over the Mississippi Valley, there could be men here from many nations.

Jean-Pierre thought that about half of the men were trappers like himself while the others were either voyageurs or keelboatmen.[73] The men of the keelboats had their own characteristic clothing, typically of linsey-woolsey and always in rough repair. He had learned long ago to give the men who worked the keelboats a wide berth if at all possible. He, like most Frenchman, liked a fight when it had to be, but would prefer an amicable settlement to any conflict. But with the keelboatmen, fighting was a pursuit. Usually, whenever they were at a place like this they were drinking heavily. All of them were strong and tough. Their life on the rivers allowed

---

73   French voyageurs were the men who propelled the French trading empire across Canada from Atlantic to the Pacific in remarkably few years. The were rivermen, highly skilled in moving large volumes of freight along the river highway. Keelboatmen, on the other hand, were typically Americans. They were also rivermen, but instead of skilled at handling the light birch bark canoes of the voyageurs, they moved the heavy keelboats down and up the southern waterways. Each group had honestly earned a reputation for strength, skill, and endurance.

for no other type of man. The men were clustered into groups of their own kind, sitting or standing in the mid-day sun, most likely talking of other days and other rivers.

Approaching the trading house, he nodded and spoke to anyone who did the same or met his eye, hoping to indicate to this crowd that he was a peace-seeking trader with no war to fight with anyone. Relief came as he passed into the shadow of the house without any challenge. But he reminded himself that he would need to be careful until he left the settlement behind him.

"Bonjour, Monsieur," called out a short, thick man from behind one of the counters. There was a smile on his face and an ease about his eyes that told Jean-Pierre that here was a man mellow in his spirit. He instantly felt good within himself about this Frenchman.

"Bonjour, Monsieur, I am Jean-Pierre Villeneuve. And I have a cargo of furs out in my pirogue. I would like to trade them if you are taking furs," he stated.

"Oui, monsieur, my name is Antoine LeFlore. And, yes, I am taking furs. All my furs will be baled to sail on one of those keel-boats within the week. I am just now waiting upon a full load. I'll give you St. Louis prices for all your prime furs. Bring them into the fur shed on the outside and I'll look through them."

"Merci, Monsieur LeFlore," replied Jean-Pierre. "It was my own father who taught me to care for furs. I have been upon the river all of my life, except for a few short years working for Monsieur Chouteau in St. Louis."[74]

---

74 Auguste Chouteau was barely fourteen years old in 1764 when he directed the building of the initial post which would later become the city of St. Louis, Missouri. He remained and built a large fur-trading empire that his sons stretched west into Kansas and Oklahoma.

"But you certainly do know your furs, if you worked for Auguste Chouteau. He has set the standard for fur traders all throughout the valley of the Mississippi," responded Monsieur LeFlore. "Come into the post and I will offer you wine to celebrate your good winter's catch."

"Merci, avec plaisir monsieur," replied Jean-Pierre with joy.

Jean-Pierre followed the trader into his post and took a chair that was offered to him. Monsieur LeFlore reached behind his counter and brought up a dark bottle, pouring some of its contents into two pewter cups. Accepting one of them, Jean-Pierre waited as his host offered a toast. "To the French, may we live on in the woods forever regardless of the English, the Spanish or the Americans," he stated with fervor. "Sante."

"Sante," responded Jean-Pierre heartily before he tasted the liquid. Startled by the quality of the flavor, he offered, "But Monsieur LeFlore, this is true French wine, is it not?"

"Mais oui, it sailed from France, a true wine from Bordeaux, to Nouvelle Orleans where I purchased a few cases of it and had it shipped to this post by keelboat. We may be many leagues from true French society, but the keelboat allows us to enjoy a bit of it here. For the American, it is enough for him to drink his home-made whiskey. But the French enjoy good wine, even here in the land of the Arkansas." Jean-Pierre had never expected to find good wine at such an isolated post. The post proprietor was taking great pride in showing off his ability to enjoy his amenities despite the isolation.

Gradually, other Frenchmen came inside to join their conversation. Jean-Pierre did note that Monsieur LeFlore did not extend the bottle to any of them. He thought that this act of charity toward himself was possibly a singular act due to the event of a trapper bringing in a remarkably good winter's catch.

Like the French back at the little settlement, these men were eager to share their tales with their own kind. The topics were about the same, but these men knew much more regarding outside events. They had been away from the lower Arkansas area and had seen things first hand. And, they had had conversations with others up and down the Fleuve Mississippi.

Jean-Pierre expressed interest in details regarding the French settlements upriver, identifying himself with Ste. Genevieve. Several men responded to his query with great tales that shook the room, even though all of these men except for Jean-Pierre had heard the stories before now.

They told of how the settlement of New Madrid had suffered great losses from the quake The level of the town was now possibly ten feet lower than previous and its cemetery had been thrown into the Fleuve Mississippi. And, the river itself had been in an uproar unknown in all the years the French, or even the Indians had been in the valley. Acres of trees were thrown into the river from above while sunken trees from the river's bottom had been thrown up to the surface. The congestion caused by these trees made the river hard to navigate.

As for the boats which happened to be on the river, many of them had been pitched up into the air by the violence of the river. Some had been washed up onto high land half a league from the river. Also, they told of lakes out in the bottom country which were drained in an instant of all their water. But, on the east side of the river, a lake was formed by the settling of the earth.[75] And, of all

---

75 This lake has been named Reelfoot and today is a favorite of area fishermen.

things, there were stories that the great river had its bottom separated creating great water falls until the soft river bottom washed even again.[76]

For hours the French boatmen talked of how the great earthquakes had desolated the middle Mississippi Valley. As a result of the three great quakes and the daily tremors, some whole communities had vanished, with no one brave enough to live in the area. Possibly the most frightening tale was of the river pirates on Island 69 who had been waiting to plunder a passing boat. The entire island had sunk into the river, taking all the pirates with it.[77] At the telling of these tales, the crowd here assembled shook their heads and called out exclamations of shock as if this were their first hearing of the accounts.

All of them begged to hear Jean-Pierre recount his own tale of the great quake. By this time they had learned that he had been alone in the Grand Marais when the initial quake struck in December. Now they listened patiently, imploring him to tell every detail. As with the Talbots, he showed himself to be a master storyteller. They one and all expressed shock at his getting out alive and agreed wholeheartedly that only God's hand could have prevented his death.

Another great event had occurred on the river during

---

76   Though doubted by some authorities, it is believed that the Mississippi River bottom separated in two places, one below and one above New Madrid, each temporarily creating a six to ten-foot waterfall across the width of the river.

77   This story, told by a river boat captain was widely accepted as truth. Island 69 was a few miles upstream from the mouth of the White River. "The Navigator" a river guide published since 1801 had maps of the Ohio and Mississippi rivers. The major islands were numbered and the direction of the currents were indicated.

Jean-Pierre's travels over the winter. It had almost eclipsed the earthquake in excitement among the white settlements and Indian villages along the Fleuve Mississippi. Part of the excitement for the Indian tribes was that this event followed the great earthquake. Two events of this magnitude occurring one after the other signified very big medicine to the local Indians who had not known anything of either kind in all of their histories.

At the same time that the first great quake had occurred in December, the first steamboat to work these inland rivers was making its maiden voyage down LaBelle Riviere. Some of the white settlers had heard of this type of boat which moved under steam power, as news from the eastern seaboard had brought many stories of such vessels. But few local residents in the mid-Mississippi valley had thought that such a craft would ever come down their rivers. The steamboat New Orleans had left Pittsburgh where it had been built and had been traveling down the La Belle Riviere when its crew first encountered people fleeing upriver to get away from the earthquake.[78]

Jean-Pierre sat mystified as some of the men relayed this story of a boat upon the great river which was powered by steam. He like the others had heard of such things but had no idea how they worked and had never expected to see one here on these inland rivers.

As during the previous nights, these Frenchmen talked late into the night, swapping stories about furs, rivers, Indians, trade and the ever repeating quakes. By the end of the evening Jean-Pierre

---

78 The New Orleans was the first steamboat to successfully ply the great inland waterways. It made round trips upriver from New Orleans to Natchez, Mississippi, having too little power to ascend the great river much farther. It was common for these craft to be named after their destination.

had developed a camaraderie with them.

It was mid-morning the next day when Jean-Pierre settled up with Monsieur LeFlore regarding his furs. He felt good about the price he was getting for the furs and decided to trade them all here at Poste aux Arkansas. He was yet undecided as to when he would return to Ste. Genevieve to visit his friends. As this point, he was quite sure none of them had been lost in the quakes as there had been few reports of deaths.

His primary need was a long firearm of some sort as it was so much more effective than a bow in dropping game. Also, along the Riviere Arkansas and the Fleuve Mississippi there was much more likelihood of encountering river pirates. Out of the used long guns available at the post, Jean-Pierre settled upon a French trade musket which was still in reasonably good condition. Also, it was priced much lower than any of the rifles.[79] With his limited resources, he did not see how he could justify the high price of a rifle. Without rifling in the barrel, the musket would not be as accurate, but it was widely known for its reliability. Simply fitted muskets of this type had been used by French and Indians for perhaps a hundred years. Also, it had one advantage over the rifle in that it could also shoot small shot for waterfowl.

As accessories for the musket, he chose several one pound-bars of lead, bullet molds for both ball and shot, a large powder horn for the barrel and a small one for the primer pan, extra flints and

---

79 Muskets, which were smooth bore military long guns, were a common item in the fur trade until the latter part of the nineteenth century. They were typically large bore, .60 caliber and larger, heavy stocked, and plainly fitted with iron. Though they did not have the longer range of a rifle, these weapons were quite sturdily built and had the advantage of being more quickly reloaded.

other incidentals necessary to the use of a firearm in the woods. He also bought a hunting pouch to carry these items.[80]

To replace the camp items lost in the earthquake, he bought a brass cooking pot, a frying pan, a small pot for boiling coffee, large flints for fire making, an extra knife and tomahawk, needles, fish-hooks and line, and a new sheet of canvas. For food, he selected flour, meal, salt and small amounts of coffee and sugar. He also purchased a pair of breeches, several pairs of moccasins, another shirt, and a felt hat. Outfitted with these few rudimentary items, Jean-Pierre could sustain himself in the wilderness for several months.

Toward mid-day two other Frenchmen, Laferty and Doudiet, proposed that he accompany them on a hunting trip up the river. They explained to him that by bringing in game every few days, the post trader did not charge as much for feeding them while they rested here. Jean-Pierre readily agreed, and the three paddled a large pirogue upriver to a stretch of high land about a league above the post. Leaving the pirogue tied to a tree at the river's edge, they separated and took their own way into the woods. It was their agreement that they would rejoin at the pirogue just after dark for the return trip to the post.

Jean-Pierre walked directly away from the river as the other

80   The operation of a flintlock rifle or musket required such accessories as a priming horn (or flask) of finely ground black gunpowder, a larger horn or flask of more coarsely ground black gunpowder for the charge in the barrel, bullets, a lubricant, a vent pick, a screwdriver, various attachments to the ramrod tip for cleaning, extra flints for the hammer, cotton or linen cloth for patches on which to seat the ball, a patch knife and other such items which individual hunters might find useful. A small amount of these items was kept in or on a hunting pouch which hung from the hunter's shoulder. Only items relating directly to the firearm were kept in the hunting pouch. A "possibles bag" for other items of personal use was a separate container and not kept on the hunter's person.

two hunters had gone downstream and upstream. Not knowing the area, he was at a loss as to trails and feeding areas. But as a woodsman he knew what signs to look for. He had been told of the Grand Prairie which was a short distance from the river and decided that this would be a good place to hunt. As quickly as he could walk without making noise, he worked his way through the woods until he found himself at the edge of a large sprawling prairie, several miles across and more miles long than he could see.[81]

At the edge of this prairie he discovered a well-traveled deer trail. Knowing nowhere else to hunt, he slipped back into the woods and secreted himself behind a large hickory. From this vantage point he remained immobile except for his eyes which moved back and forth ever so slowly, searching for any movement that might belong to a deer. On this trip, hunting small game was not their intent as it would require too many to fill the needs of the large number of men back at the post.

Scarcely fifteen minutes had passed when Jean-Pierre glanced to his left and saw two deer heading toward the woods. Mentally readying himself, he sensed through his hands the shape of the flintlock musket which he had only fired in practice. When the deer turned somewhat to their left, he eased himself around into

81   Grand Prairie was a grassland prairie mostly void of trees. Nuttall, an English scholar who traveled through the region in 1819, indicated that it stretched several miles wide and about sixty miles in length, roughly paralleling the White River. Records today suggest that this prairie region extended northwesterly as far as the present town of Searcy, Arkansas, some ninety miles. It is thought that this prairie existed due to a dense underlying silty clay soil which prevented the penetration of water. Tree roots could not penetrate this barrier though grasses that grew above it were prolific. Today it proves excellent for rice production. Prairies were extremely rare in the southern woodlands, but they did exist. A few small prairies existed in southeastern Missouri.

a shooting position. Now raising the long gun, he pulled back the large, curved hammer. Jean-Pierre pointed the barrel toward an opening in the brush where he believed the two deer would cross his line of sight. As the forward one walked clearly into this opening, he lined up the sights above the barrel just behind the animal's front shoulder and squeezed the trigger. The curved hammer fell forward bringing the flint against the frizzen. A shower of sparks went down into the pan filled with powder. With a bright flash, this powder burst into flame, igniting the powder leading into the rear of the barrel. An explosion rocked the heavy long gun as a huge billow of blue gray smoke rushed out of the end of the barrel.

In the seconds it took for the smoke to clear, Jean-Pierre saw one of the deer spring forward into the woods to his right. In those same seconds, he followed a long practiced procedure of reloading the flintlock. First, powder was poured from the powder measure down the barrel. Then, a lead ball on a patch of greased linen cloth was placed atop the end of the barrel and forced down by the use of the ramrod which fitted in the stock underneath the barrel. Next, a small measure of the finer priming powder was sprinkled into the pan. All this was done quickly but methodically in anticipation of any danger.

By now the smoke had cleared, and Jean-Pierre was able to see one deer lying in the prairie grass. Knowing the nature of deer, he eased himself carefully and quietly to his right in search of the second deer. It was the routine of deer in such a situation that the deer not shot would stop nearby and wait upon the one which had remained behind. This was what Jean-Pierre was counting on.

A moment later, he saw the second deer standing just inside the edge of the woods, looking back for its companion. Jean-Pierre carefully worked himself through the undergrowth until the animal's left front shoulder was clearly visible. Taking a quick but deliberate aim, he fired a large lead ball into the deer's chest.

While the smoke cleared, he repeated the reloading process before stepping forward. This time he took the time to swab out the barrel before reloading. Only then did he go to investigate his shots. At each deer he checked the entrance wound and slit the animal's throat. Jean-Pierre was gratified to know that each shot had struck true. Glancing briefly at the musket, he spoke aloud, "Mon ami, you shoot true to the mark." Despite knowing that the musket would not hold its accuracy at the longer ranges like a rifle, Jean-Pierre felt good about his recent purchase. Surely, it would get him by until a rifle could be gained in trade.

He gutted the two deer, leaving the carcasses to cool in the coming night air. He knew that at this time his two companions had not brought down game as there had been no shots other than his own. Not yet ready to begin the walk back through the woods with one of the deer, he decided to walk out on the prairie. This location would not be good for hunting now after the noise and smell of powder, as well as the smell of blood.

It was getting late and light was failing quickly, but Jean-Pierre wanted to see something more of this grassy area. After a time, several deer appeared in the distance. Standing there, he debated as to whether he should kill another as the capacity of the pirogue was limited. But as he had still heard no other shots, he knew that his companions had been unsuccessful. Also, he reminded himself that there would not be light much longer for any of them. With this conclusion, he crouched down and waited for the deer to pass by, using the tall grasses and bushes to conceal himself.

When within about fifty yards, Jean-Pierre feared that he would be detected by one of the small herd. Until now a light wind had covered his scent and the sounds of his approach. Lying on his belly, he sighted carefully along the barrel at the closest deer. The dim light showed a bright shower of sparks out from the barrel when the shot was squeezed off. At this, the herd bounded away into the closing darkness of the night. Rising to one knee, Jean-Pierre reloaded the musket before moving forward. Only now did he step forward to search out his possible kill. Having lived his entire life in the woods where both animal and human enemies could be hiding just out of sight, he never moved without a loaded weapon.

Somewhat to his surprise, his third shot had been as successful as his first two. A young buck lay in the grass, gasping its last breaths. With his long knife, Jean-Pierre opened its throat to drain the carcass quickly of blood before gutting it. With the deer over his shoulders and his loaded musket ready in his right hand, he quickly strode back toward the other carcasses.

Almost back to the edge of the woods, he heard the cry of an owl, but with an extra end note. He replied in kind and continued his direction of travel, repeating the call after a time to indicate to the first caller his direction of travel. Near the first kill, Laferty, who had hunted upriver, came through the darkness and congratulated him for the deer on his shoulders. "It is so good, Jean-Pierre, that you bring in a deer while I got nothing, but did it take you three shots for just one deer?" asked Laferty in jest.

"Non, mon ami," replied Jean-Pierre with a smile, "one shot for this deer and one each for the other two," pointing out the others with the barrel of his musket.

"Oh, now I see, at least I get to carry one back, even if I did not shoot one," laughed Laferty.

Another owl call close by warned them that Doudiet was walking toward them in the darkness.

By this time, Laferty had lifted a deer to his own shoulders. "Doudiet, there is one for you as well. Jean-Pierre here would not leave you out of the work," cheerfully called out Laferty. With this manner of jest, the three hunters carried their burdens through the thickness of the dark woods to where their pirogue was tied. Jean-Pierre led the way as he had walked through these woods earlier. With unerring direction, he led his companions out of the woods to within fifty feet of the pirogue, causing them much surprise.

Later at the post, the three deer were hung on a high pole for final cleaning, skinning, and butchering. Some of the Frenchmen who had remained at the post attended to these chores, allowing the hunters to rest and have a cup of coffee. This was a time for retelling the hunt. Laftery and Doudiet did the retelling though Jean-Pierre had actually done the killing. Each of them told of Jean-Pierre's prowess as a hunter and as a navigator, exaggerating whenever possible. As the meat was sliced off the carcasses and laid over the cook fires, some of the Americans passed a jug of whiskey around as their offering for the meal. Such was the stuff of campfires of men in the wilderness.

When Jean-Pierre arose the next morning, he found himself being sought out by one of the clerks from the post. This man informed him that Monsieur LeFlore wanted to see him in his quarters. Jean-Pierre followed the clerk through the post into the rear of the building. Here Monsieur LeFlore occupied a large bed in a spacious room with furnishings more like those found in a city than in an isolated outpost.

"Bonjour, Monsieur Villeneuve, I trust you are well this morning," stated Monsieur LeFlore.

"Oui, Monsieur, but what of you, are you feeling ill?" asked Jean-Pierre.

"Oui, unfortunately. It is the gout, I fear. It seems to come and go on its own. For sure, I prefer its going to its coming. The most unfortunate part is its timing. I was due to set sail for Nouvelle Orleans in two days with my furs on Monsieur MacDuff's keelboat. But, now, that is out of the question as the pain is too much to bear. I just cannot travel at this time," explained Monsieur LeFlore.

"I gather there is something that I might do for you, that you sent for me this morning," stated Jean-Pierre.

"Oui, something very important," answered Monsieur LeFlore. He paused now to adjust his right leg which was elevated upon the footboard. Jean-Pierre waited patiently as the trader's expression displayed the great pain which was passing. In a moment, the trader found sufficient relief to continue. Slowly, he now spoke, "I believe I knew your father. I was an apprentice clerk under a trader in St. Louis when your father arrived after a winter's trade upon the Riviere Chariton. Your mother was with him, and you as well. You must have been only about ten years old. What I particularly remember is that instead of individually inspecting the furs as was my trader's usual insistence, he instructed me to take the count from your father as he gave it, as his word was sufficient. I remember that clearly now, and I believe that you, Jean-Pierre, are also such a man."

Jean-Pierre had listened with pride at the reference to his father's honor among traders but had inwardly winced at the mention of the Riviere Chariton. "Merci beaucoup, monsieur, for your kind words about my father. It is quite kind of you," responded Jean-Pierre.

"Jean-Pierre," spoke Monsieur LeFlore," I find myself needing to prevail upon your honor and upon your generosity. Would you be so kind as to travel with my furs to Nouvelle Orleans to act as my agent in their sale and the purchase of the supplies which I need for trade throughout the coming summer? Normally they are brought down from Canada, but this trip I will get them at Nouvelle Orleans."

Somewhat startled, Jean-Pierre paused before answering, "Monsieur, it is such a kind offer, but I have never done such a task. I'm not certain that I could do you a good service in such a matter." "In your many years on the rivers and dealings with traders at the different posts, I'm sure you have gained the necessary skills. And, from what I have seen and heard of you in the short time you have been here at Poste aux Arkansas, I would have all the faith in you as my agent," declared Monsieur LeFlore.

Jean-Pierre hesitated at such a responsibility on someone's else's behalf. But he admitted to himself that he eagerly anticipated seeing Nouvelle Orleans. Jean-Pierre then responded, "If this is your wish, Monsieur, then I will do it. And, I assure you that I will honor your faith in me."

Happy with this agreement, Monsieur LeFlore took some time to give certain instructions about what needed to be done prior to the departure of the keelboat. He further stated that the clerks at the post would take care of most of the preparations. It was important that Jean-Pierre clearly understand what was expected of him while in Nouvelle Orleans.

Chapter Seven

Nouvelle Orleans

It was late in the morning when Jean-Pierre left Poste aux Arkansas for Nouvelle Orleans. Though he had seen keelboats before, this was the first time he had ever been aboard one. This keelboat was painted a dark red and its name, *The Lassie*, was printed in heavy black letters on the bow. It was about fifty feet long and ten feet wide carrying a single mast and sail.

It was also the first time for him to act as an agent for another in such a large venture. The whole experience made him anxious, very unlike setting out in a pirogue to trade and trap furs by himself on some lonely waterway.

The weather was fair and windy on this late March day. The crew of the keelboat poled and rowed the craft into the main current, which would help carry them downstream. The river was much lower than when Jean-Pierre had paddled his pirogue upstream the week before. It was now within its banks, though there was still a reddish color to the water that Jean-Pierre assumed would not be there during normal flow.[82]

Sitting on the cabin in the middle of the craft, Jean-Pierre

82 The Arkansas River is the fifth longest waterway in the United States, draining snow water from the Rocky Mountains and the overflow waters of fourteen hundred miles of varied terrain between. The reddish tint during some of the flood stages was from the Canadian and Cimarron rivers which joined the Arkansas in present day Oklahoma.

went over in his mind all the items that Monsieur LeFlore was sending to Nouvelle Orleans. There were many bales of furs, including beaver, raccoon, and mink, as well as a great many deer and bear hides. Each bale held only one type of pelt and had been compressed by the fur press before being bound with rawhide straps. The compressed bales would take up less space in the hold. Other items on board were casks of honey and bear oil, both highly valued on the frontier and in ports such as Nouvelle Orleans. In addition to the pelts and casks, salted deer and bear hams made up a large share of the load. Several casks of pecans from upriver were also aboard.

Even though Jean-Pierre carried papers detailing the entire load, he also kept Monsieur LeFlore's cargo in his mind. He had never learned much about reading and writing, so like most trappers and traders, he depended upon his memory. But this load was so large that Jean-Pierre was very thankful that the paper he carried had everything written down. However, he knew that he would go over these goods again and again in his head during the voyage. Of course, he had little else to do as he was not part of the crew but would simply sit by and watch the progress of the craft.

He had gotten to know something about the crew during the loading of Monsieur LeFlore's cargo. Now he observed them at length in their natural environment on the river. The Patroon was a Scotchman named Angus MacDuff, a man of medium height and stocky build. He had long bushy sideburns and a bushy mustache, all showing enough gray for him to be well past middle age. He appeared to be a good natured man, but prone to raucous outbursts when excited. Jean-Pierre speculated that he had spent his earlier years as part of a crew and at some point acquired enough resources to purchase his own keelboat.

This crew was a motley group of fourteen men, some large, and some not so large; all ill dressed in ragged linsey-woolsey[83] and a variety of hats to match their different backgrounds. All were tempered by hard living and hard work. Traveling the rivers of the Mississippi Valley was often a lonely life. It took a great deal of time between settlements, and longer yet before returning to a home port. Being pressed together on a small craft often caused tense moments. More often than not, these were settled with blood, mostly from fists but sometimes from long sharp knives. There were occasions when some of a keelboat crew did not complete the whole trip.

It was easy enough going downriver for the current did most of the work. But Jean-Pierre knew that working their way back upstream would be a different story as the craft would have to be rowed, poled, or pulled the entire way, around every bend, across every current, and off many sandbars. Sometimes the sail would be of benefit out on a wide river like the Mississippi, but it was not dependable and was never enough. Though thieves were a constant problem for river travelers, most river pirates avoided keelboats as they were heavily manned with men as tough as themselves.

By this time the crew had come to accept Jean-Pierre. They had quickly learned that he was a man of substance, capable and skilled in the ways of the woods and rivers, and an intelligent organizer. They had seen that he sought not to crowd anyone, but instead chose to work with those around him. So he sat on the cabin, taking in the scene around him—the boat, the crew and the river around them.

As the hours passed, the craft quickly moved downstream.

---

83 Linsey-woolsey was a composite of linen and wool, the cloth of common laborers.

To aid the work of the current, Monsieur MacDuff had eight men at the oars, pulling hard. Jean-Pierre wondered if the reason was additional speed or to restore discipline to the strong-minded crew. They had grown lazy and ill tempered during their rest at Poste aux Arkansas. At any rate, they moved downstream at probably three leagues and hour, carrying approximately fifteen tons of freight from Poste aux Arkansas and camps farther up the Riviere Arkansas.

By mid-afternoon, they passed the overflow outlet which allowed excess water from the Arkansas to flow toward the Blanche. At nightfall, they had not reached the mouth of the Arkansas, but Monsieur MacDuff did not stop. Instead, he took a position at the bow and called back directions to the rudder. Jean-Pierre was not concerned as he believed that this man knew the river intimately and could guide them safely in daylight or darkness. Besides, the craft was not a light pirogue. If the keelboat struck a log or a sand bar, it would not crack or turn over easily for it was heavily constructed with most of its weight below to give it stability.

Jean-Pierre sat on the cabin and smoked his pipe, taking in the actions and words around him. His English was good enough to catch most things which were said, the rest he determined from the situation. He could have gone below and slept, but this experience was exhilarating.

Sometime in the night, they came to the mouth of the Arkansas, a wide expanse at its juncture with the Flueve Mississippi. At Monsieur MacDuff's direction, the boss guided the keelboat to the right and downstream into the main current of the great river.[84] Even in the light of a full moon, Jean-Pierre could not begin

---

84 The second-in-command on a keelboat was called "boss." He normally worked the bow. The word is possibly a derivative of "boatswain's

to determine the width of the river. The crew was given leave to take their night's rest. Some sprawled on the deck while others went below. Jean-Pierre followed those below to rest among the bales of fur. Now only Monsieur MacDuff and the boss guided the craft.

Jean-Pierre awoke just after first light despite the lateness of his falling asleep. Drawing himself up to the roof of the cabin, he gazed with wonder at the great river, almost one third of a league across here. There was a light morning fog on the water. One of the crew, a man called Hutton, was at the bow, and another whose name Jean-Pierre could not remember was at the rudder. The crew guided the craft down the river in shifts, rarely stopping, as the river was familiar to the crew. Heavy spring rains had the great river at flood stage, allowing the keelboat to float over much of the land which had formed the bends. The strong current and this shortening of distance made for a fast pace. At this rate, they could possibly travel seventy leagues a day. He believed that at this rate they would be in Nouvelle Orleans in just a few days. Occasionally they saw isolated cabins or small settlements on the higher banks. As these held no interest for the crew, the keelboat continued downriver toward Nouvelle Orleans.

A few days after entering the Fleuve Mississippi, they sighted Natchez[85] on their left bank. Monsieur MacDuff directed that they

---

mate," a warrant or petty officer on ship

85 Natchez, Mississippi had been a stop-over point for rivermen for many years. Flatboatmen usually walked back upstream from New Orleans to Natchez before taking the overland route (The Natchez Trace) to Nashville. Keelboatmen and flatboatmen alike enjoyed this stop on the river. The town, which sat high on the bluff, maintained some state of the decorum expected in a city of wealth. The riverfront, "Natchez under the hill" was a riotous company of gamblers, prostitutes, whiskey purveyors and other thieves. Here the rivermen found entertainment after the boredom and hard toil of weeks of life on the river. Residents of this

pass on by without a stop. His decision quickly brought a torrent of groans and oaths from a crew that had looked forward to stopping at Natchez. Jean-Pierre had heard much of Natchez over the years but had never been this far south. It was a rowdy river boat town supporting a thriving economy based on the sale of cotton and indigo, and also on gambling and prostitution. This was always a favorite port of the rivermen. It sat high on a bluff with its landing crowded with river craft, almost as if it were beckoning to the crew of *The Lassie*.

Monsieur MacDuff promised all the liquor they could drink in Nouvelle Orleans and to stop in Natchez on the return trip. This did little to quiet the discontent. Voices continued to rise, and a mutiny seemed certain. Jean-Pierre began to tense as he saw anger rising from every quarter. Just then, the patroon turned to face the crew with his thumbs hitched in his wide belt and his shoulders thrown back. His head shook left and right, causing his hair to fly about. Everyone saw the wild look in his eyes as he stood there, tensed, daring any or all to actually defy him. One by one the crew slowly returned to their duties and no more was spoken of the matter. Jean-Pierre wondered how severe Monsieur MacDuff could be if his hot-headed crew could be subdued with only a stare.

The trip down the Mississippi was a pleasant one for Jean-Pierre. The great river was so wide that it was hard to see objects on the shore clearly as they passed down its middle. He noticed the weather warming day by day as they traveled south and also changes in the vegetation. Spanish moss became a common sight on the cypress along the river's edge.

---

quarter were not allowed to ascend the hill to the town proper.

On the evening after they passed Natchez, the crew became more mellow. Monsieur MacDuff had opened a fresh jug of whiskey and passed it around freely. This served to cause them to forget Natchez as well as to loosen their tongues into song. The fiddler had begun to pull tunes from the strings, and the men joined in with the familiar songs.

Jean-Pierre was surprised by the wide repertoire of songs known by these rough boatmen. On thinking about it, he reminded himself that his own fellow voyageurs were known for their many songs sang during their long days at the paddle. He enjoyed this time with these keelboatmen, joining in with their singing as he learned the words and tunes.

> Some rows up, but we rows down,
> All the way to Shawnee town,
> Pull away—pull away!

> Oh! It's love was the 'casion of my downfall,
> I wish I hadn't never loved none at all!
> Oh! It's love was the 'casion of my miserre;
> Now I am bound, but once I was free.

Some would be sung in parts, with one side answering the other.

> "Where you from?"
> "Redstone."
> "What's you lading?"
> "Millstones."
> "Who's your captain?"

"Whetstone."

"Where're you bound?"

"Limestone."

Jean-Pierre became so caught up in their spirit that during a lull in the music, he shared one of the river songs of his countrymen.

> Dans mon Chemin j'ai recontre
> Trois cavalieres bien montees,
> L'on, ton, laridon, danee
> L'on, ton, laridon, dai.

> Trois cavalieres bien montees
> L'une a cheval, l'autre a pied,
> L'on, ton, laridon, danee
> L'on, ton, laridon, dai.[86]

At noon on the tenth day out of Poste aux Arkansas, *The Lassie* landed at Nouvelle Orleans, Jean-Pierre found himself at the threshold of a large and bustling city, The length of the landing along the river's edge was packed with every type of river craft that he had ever known. There were keelboats, flatboats, bateaux, pirogues, and rafts. Most of the keelboats were brightly painted, but the flatboats were weathered gray from their single trip down the river. But what caught Jean-Pierre's eye were the tall sailing

---

86 The song is loosely translated from the French as "In my path, I met three horsewomen, well mounted." The remainder of the verse, as well as the second half of the second verse, is gibberish, like "da da da, de de de." The second verse reads "Three horsewomen well mounted, the one on a horse, the others afoot."

ships which had undoubtedly crossed an ocean before arriving at Nouvelle Orleans. Boats and more boats stretched farther than he could see down the river. He knew that this Nouvelle Orleans was the grandest city he had ever seen.

Monsieur MacDuff was kind enough to show Jean-Pierre around the landing, introducing him to men he knew to be trustworthy. The crew took shifts standing guard over the keelboat day and night while its cargo was being sold and another bought. In this manner, some of the crew would always be with the boat. He told Jean-Pierre of the many thieves in Nouvelle Orleans and that a man could not step away from his goods for any time at all. Jean-Pierre appreciated the patroon's diligence as by himself he could not possibly protect Monsieur LeFlore's cargo while seeking out buyers and sellers at the same time.

All the crew who were not assigned to guard *The Lassie* set about having a rowdy time in the drinking establishments of an area known as "the swamp." Jean-Pierre and Monsieur MacDuff walked to one of the large warehouses that bought goods from upriver. They located Monsieur Jean Lieux, the agent whom Monsieur LeFlore had directed him to contact regarding buying the cargo from Poste aux Arkansas. Monsieur MacDuff also regularly dealt with this man regarding that portion of the cargo which belonged to him.

Monsieur Lieux expressed regret at the news of Monsieur LeFlore's gout and wished Jean-Pierre to convey his sympathy. With the papers delivered regarding the cargo, Jean-Pierre felt relieved to have one burden lifted from him. Now he could focus on purchasing the trade goods for the return trip.

This task could not be hurried and would take several weeks. Prices had to be agreed on to sell the furs. Trade goods and supplies had to be inspected carefully for quality, and price negotiations sometimes took place over several days. As the cargo was sold, it was unloaded and stored. Jean-Pierre felt that he should attend to this personally even though the warehouse workers did the actual work. It was very important to him that all Monsieur LeFlore's cargo be counted and given full credit.

Monsieur LeFlore needed goods to trade during the coming year to keelboatmen, voyageurs, American settlers, and to the Indian parties that frequently traveled by Poste aux Arkansas. The list he trusted to Jean-Pierre included blankets, casks of flour, meal, gunpowder, molasses, spices, mirrors, needles, whiskey, wine, boxes of bar lead, axes, flints, strikers, traps, pots, pans, kettles, and many incidental items.

Since Jean-Pierre was acting as a purchasing agent for Poste aux Arkansas, he could purchase everything at prices much lower than in any of the settlements upriver. He decided to use the Spanish bits he had received from Monsieur LeFlore to make some purchases for himself. Perhaps having the same first name as Monsieur Lieux, owner of the warehouse, helped in that matter. Jean-Pierre chose a brightly decorated white linen shirt and indigo dyed breeches made of the best material. He also selected items such as a mirror, more traps, extra flints, powder, salt, vermillion, a colorful tuque, a red sash, plus numerous incidental personal items which he normally did without. There was something about surviving the previous winter that put him a festive mood.

On a few occasions over the past years, he had owned pistols but had always traded them for something he needed more at the time. But times were quickly changing. Thieves and murderers were becoming a constant threat. In places along the Flueve Mississippi or along the Natchez Trace, they worked in packs like wolves. Jean-Pierre believed that it was only a matter of time before he became a target of such a group. And, of course, there were always the Osage. His blood warmed at the thought of his old enemies.

Jean-Pierre asked Monsieur Lieux about pistols. At the inquiry, he brought out a brace of dueling pistols for Jean-Pierre's inspection. Then he related the story that a wealthy Creole lady had turned them over to him for disposal after her husband had died from wounds suffered in a duel behind the Cathedral.[87] Monsieur Lieux offered them to Jean-Pierre for so little that refusal was out of the question.

The two matched pistols came in an ornate wooden box, resting in velvet lined cavities, and surrounded by numerous accessories. The .46 caliber barrels were seven inches long. He appreciated their graceful European styling of richly polished wood decorated with silver, much preferred over the heavy American pistols which were available in St. Louis. Beyond their beauty, he looked to the time when these might save his life or the life of one of his companions.

Here, Jean-Pierre arranged his weapons; the Pennsylvania rifle, the French musket, the brace of pistols and his ash bow. Of course, he always carried a long knife and tomahawk. In close quarters, these weapons had proven in times

As busy as he was, Jean-Pierre found some time to explore the city. Of all the marvels of this great city, he found the street lights to be the most fascinating. Large oil lamps hung on every

---

87   Code Duello was the European code of honor which ruled the fighting of duels. In New Orleans, these duels were customarily fought behind the church at dawn.

street corner. Such a thing he had never heard of, much less seen for himself. The many beautiful houses seemed endless. Decorative balconies, iron grillwork, fountains, courtyards, and gardens were common. But as beautiful as he found the city, he was uncomfortable with the crowds. So many people made him anxious.

So he mostly kept by the river where the warehouses and the landing were located. He believed that this was enough city for him and he was a little bit afraid that if he got too far from the landing, he would be unable to find his way back. This was a new feeling to a man who could find his way through any wilderness. But all the people and their houses made him nervous.

Being Monsieur LeFlore's agent took most of his attention, but he was able to spend some time with the crew. By the time he was able to join them in their revelry, most of them had been drunk for two days. He also enjoyed an opportunity to celebrate, but on this occasion, he was restrained because of his obligations.

Jean-Pierre was as uncomfortable in the Swamp as he had been in the crowded streets and beautiful buildings of the town. This part of the city was largely drinking establishments and gambling dens for the keelboat and flatboat crews. Occasionally there was a boarding house, and they all were made of dismantled flatboats. There were little or no decorations, and a stench of liquor and sweat permeated the air. Violence and theft were commonplace. Typically, the local law did not venture into the Swamp after dark.

One night Jean-Pierre had retired to their boarding house earlier than the crew. He was sound asleep when he heard a thundering roar of stomping feet and bellowing voice. Instantly, he sat up in bed wide awake with one of his new pistols in hand. When Monsieur MacDuff broke through the door, his face showed a mixture of rage and desperation.

In an angry and panicky voice, he shouted out, "Mister Villernew, we're in real mess this time. Yes, we are. Ya'see, the crew has gotten inter a drunken brawl with some local 'gentlemen' and have been thrown into the Calaboso. It twern't enough thet they tore up a whole saloon. But the situation was much worsened when O'Sullivan, you yourself know what a particularly hot-headed Irishman he is, well, sir, he opened up one of the local favorites with his blade. Now the whole crew will have to stand trial, and *The Lassie* could be tied up here for months."Immediately feeling himself drawn in by the magnitude of the problem, Jean-Pierre anxiously asked, "What are you planning to do, Monsieur?"

Somewhat calmed now by the sharing of the bad news with the Frenchman, the Patroon spoke with a calm certainty. "Wal, sir, I reckon thar's jest one thang I can do, an's thet's ta' break open thet that Calaboso this very night and set sail immediately. Once up river, we would be safe from any New Orleans law."

The whole thing sounded risky to Jean-Pierre, as he had seen the Calaboso and knew it to be a formidable structure. But he knew the patroon to be a man of great resolve and ability and supposed that with daring it could be accomplished.

"But, Monsieur," queried Jean-Pierre with great concern, "What about our cargo. We have not loaded what we have purchased. I cannot return to Poste aux Arkansas without the goods Monsieur LeFlore needs for his trade."

"I've a'ready thought thet out," stated the Patroon, pressing a sack of coins into Jean-Pierre's hand, "Ya finish making the purchases and set sail on the steamboat. It's due to sail fer Natchez in a few weeks. If'en we git to Natchez 'fore ya', we'll wait thar'. An' if'en ya beat us, ya do the same. We'll join up at 'Natchez under the hill'."

The plan seemed to be workable, thought Jean-Pierre, though there could also be great risks. And now he felt the responsibility for the property of two men, and he would be alone in Nouvelle Orleans to complete the purchases. With an uneasy feeling, he agreed as he saw no other way.

"Oui, Monsieur, Jean-Pierre will do his best for you." agreed a somewhat reluctant Jean-Pierre.

With relief in his voice, Monsieur MacDuff replied, "Thanky, Mister Villernew, now ya stay on her' as it wouldn't be good for either of us if anyone saw ya' with me before or during the breakout." With those words, Monsieur MacDuff left to rescue his crew, and with them his boat.

He walked quickly to a local stable and "borrowed" three yoke of oxen. He drove the oxen to a grilled window behind the jail. Whispered words through the window located the crew in the darkness and the Patroon informed them of the plan. A chain was quickly hitched to the iron grill. With a loud call and a sharp jab, the oxen's six tons of muscle and bone snapped the chain tight. A large section of the wall of the Calaboso was torn away and dragged down the street as the oxen received no command to stop.

As soon as the wall fell, everyone in the jail, including the crew of *The Lassie*, wasted no time in scrambling through the rubble to freedom. Though some of the crew were still drunk and half asleep, they understood the urgency of the moment. Using the most poorly lighted streets, the Patroon led the way through the shadows to the landing. There they took no time at all in poling *The Lassie* into the darkness of the great river.

Immediately, the angry Patroon set eight men to the oars, giving them sharp commands in hushed tones as they did not want to attract attention. To make their escape complete, they needed to slip from the landing into the darkness of the river as soon as possible. Once totally out of sight and hearing of the landing, Monsieur MacDuff ordered the remaining crew to raise the sail, hoping a night breeze would speed their retreat upriver.

Upon waking in the morning and going out for his coffee, Jean-Pierre heard all about the rowdy men of the river. The streets were full of talk about all the prisoners escaping from the Calaboso in the middle of the night. Some of the ones already captured had stated that it was a keelboat crew who had broken open the wall. Now their boat was missing from the landing and it there was much speculation that they had gone back upriver.

While the local officials were loudly promising to go after the crew, they faced the immediate need to recapture the many other prisoners. Some of these were quite dangerous, including a few murderers. But the owner of the saloon knew that the possibility of confronting an entire keelboat crew on their own river while they were sober might be more dangerous than the city officials would risk. Their opinion was that after the threats were made and the other prisoners brought back to the Calaboso, the incident would be forgotten. Such was the price of commerce in Nouvelle Orleans.

Jean-Pierre himself feigned complete surprise at the events. He spoke loud and long about the position in which these Americans had placed him as now he had no way to ship his goods back upriver. This passionate pretense quickly drew sympathy from the local citizens of Nouvelle Orleans, even though some of them had seen him with Monsieur MacDuff and the crew. Some even suggested he ship his goods upriver as far as Natchez on the *New Orleans*.[88] After reaching Natchez, he surely could find a reliable keelboat crew to continue the journey. Agreeing that this was excellent advice and thanking them for their kindness, Jean-Pierre immediately set about finishing his purchases.

Regardless of their fatigue or drunkenness, the keelboat Patroon drove his rowdy crew through the remainder of the night and all the next morning. He berated them as a troublesome bunch of brawlers who had cost him greatly by their wildness. Not only was his business left unfinished, but his boat would not be welcome in New Orleans again for a long time. When tempers had cooled and memories somewhat dulled, they might consider trading again at the port. In the meantime, *The Lassie* could come no farther downriver than Natchez. Further, leaving New Orleans with an empty hold upset him even more. Never had he had to do such a thing. The only consolation was that the empty craft assisted their hasty retreat upriver.

Finally, at about mid-day, he directed the craft in behind a long island that lay near the east bank. Finding a place well screened by young willows, they tied off to rest. A lookout was posted on the crest of the island to watch for any possible pursuit. Two men had

---

88   As mentioned in chapter 6, The New Orleans, the first steamboat to work the Mississippi River system, had too little power to overcome the strong current of the great river much farther upstream than Natchez, Mississippi. Built in Pittsburgh at a cost of $40,000, it earned one half of that back the first season. It had been moving down the Ohio River toward New Orleans when the Great Earthquake occurred and had arrived there only a few months prior to our character's ride upon it. Its regular run was from New Orleans to Natchez, with stops in between. It carried manufactured goods and processed foods upriver and cotton, indigo, and other crops downriver. It also carried a variety of passengers; laborers, merchants, traders, planters, and gamblers. The round trip took seventeen days. It sank in 1814 after hitting a snag.

been chosen earlier in the morning for this duty. They had been allowed to sleep a few hours while the rest of the crew rowed upriver. Now everyone else could sleep until after nightfall. Exhausted, they soon fell asleep on the deck.

But with nightfall, the crew would be awakened and ordered back into service. It was still important to increase their distance from Nouvelle Orleans. The Patroon would not feel safe until reaching Natchez. He believed that no justice-seeking group from New Orleans would dare try to remove them from Natchez. Their fear would be that every keelboat and flatboat crew, as well as a good share of the locals from Natchez 'under the hill,' would set upon them. Should that happen, the crowd from New Orleans would quickly return downriver.

As instructed, one of the guards returned to wake MacDuff shortly after dark. The guards had managed to stay awake out of fear of what would happen to them if they were caught asleep by their Patroon. On a previous occasion, he had beaten and whipped a night guard almost into unconsciousness for falling asleep on post. That memory was brought back fresh to the guards. They had agreed with one another that the stakes were much higher now and his mood was not compassionate.

In the darkness, the Patroon slipped over the side of the boat into the shallows. He washed away the remainder of the sleep by sloshing water over his head. He stood there in the faint light of a quarter moon, dripping water from his shaggy head like an angered bull. His memory of the previous evening and why they had left New Orleans in the darkness with their tails tucked was still fresh. Presently, he walked up on the island and conferred with the guard. Here he received a report that there did not seem to be any danger to them out on the river.

Pleased but not happy, he returned to the boat and began to wake the crew, quietly, but not pleasantly. He allowed them only about ten minutes to refresh themselves before he ordered the boat untied. Everyone knew that this meant to get on or be left. The only allowance made for food was to pass deerskin bags of parched corn and jerky in the few minutes before their departure.[89] Truly, he still was in no mood for leniency.

The cordelle[90] was let out, and six men towed the craft through the shallow water and bushes out to where they might rejoin the main channel. The others were ordered to the poles. When they reached the main channel, it was the slow routine of the night before, steadily rowing upstream. The progress on this upstream trip was dramatically slower and much more laborious than had been on their trip down.

Over the next few weeks, Jean-Pierre was able to complete purchasing the supplies for Monsieur LeFlore and Monsieur MacDuff. During this time he supervised loading his purchases on

---

89   Dried foods, both vegetable and animal, were often staples of frontiersmen. These foods were light, took up little space, and were for the most part non-perishable.

90   A cordelle was a long thick rope used by the keelboat crew to draw the heavily laden boat upstream when the current was too strong for the oars and too deep for the poles. In shallow water, the crew waded, but when it was deep, they trudged along the shore, fighting their way around brush and through mud. Snakes were a common problem. The poles were long and straight, and with an iron point for longer wear. They were used both to propel and to guide the craft upstream.

the steamboat. While on board the New Orleans to supervise his cargo, he looked over this marvel of the waterways. Built of wood, the craft was about 140 feet long with a thirty-foot beam and was two stories above the water line. On the front of the upper level was an open deck where passengers had a view of the river. Two masts carried sails for extra speed.[91] Being relatively new, it was brightly painted and stood out at the landing.

On the day of its departure from the landing at Nouvelle Orleans, a large crowd had gathered to see it off. Huge columns of gray smoke had been belching from the round black pipes for about an hour as the boiler built up a head of steam. It required a great deal of steam pressure to move this large craft against the powerful current of the great river.

Jean-Pierre found himself tightly clutching the rail, apprehensive about what might happen. A whistle was blown several times sharply, and the lines holding the craft were loosened from their posts. Suddenly the giant paddle wheel at the rear began to turn, creating a great splash. After a few seconds of this spinning and splashing, the *New Orleans* began to move away from the landing and turned into the main river. After about an hour of steady progress upriver without an explosion or fire or sinking, Jean-Pierre began to relax. Then he realized that he enjoyed the sensation of standing high above the surface of the river while moving against the current. He as yet did not understand the machine, but thought it was an exciting experience.

Jean-Pierre, typical of the Mississippi Valley French, was a

---

91   Later steamboats used no sails, but like the keelboats, their crew used nautical terms as they both were an extension of maritime commerce. In time and usage, the terms were often localized.

jovial sort, and he mixed well with the other passengers. He found them to be a collection of settlers, businessmen, traders, cotton planters, workmen, and gamblers. He met and chatted with several passengers at length, getting to know something of their lives. Yet he always had an eye for the river. His lifetime of river travel had disciplined him always to watch the river, the stretch ahead, the old channels, the animals, the changes in vegetation and the edges of the banks. Each and every detail was judged for value or danger and stored away for future use. During his visits with the other passengers, he had noticed the meeting or passing of flatboats and keelboats, as well as the variety of vegetation and wildlife not common to the middle and upper Mississippi. There was a great deal of Spanish Moss hanging from the limbs of the cypress, and alligators were often observed lying along the bank.

As the *New Orleans* steamed its way up to the landing at Natchez, Jean-Pierre was anxious to locate his keelboat friends. Even before the steamboat was tied off securely, he had spotted *The Lassie* among the many other river craft. Quickly slipping off the boat before the deck became cluttered with people, Jean-Pierre went directly to the keelboat. There he found O'Sullivan, morosely standing guard. Apparently, he had been assigned all the guard duty in Natchez while they waited upon the *New Orleans* to bring Jean-Pierre and their cargo upriver.

With the sense of command which had been thrust upon him over the past weeks, Jean-Pierre questioned O'Sullivan regarding Monsieur MacDuff and the remainder of the crew. "Monsieur O'Sullivan, where is Monsieur MacDuff?"

With something of a snarl the surly Irishman replied, "Off to the Blue Nose tavern, prob'bly gettin' drunk and havin' a grand ol' time."

"Is his business here in Natchez complete?" pressed Jean-Pierre who was anxious to get Monsieur LeFlore's good upriver before anything else happened.

"Yeah, he's all ready to go, soon's ya git her'," responded O'Sullivan."Then I will go and bring them back so we can load our good," stated Jean-Pierre. With rough directions from O'Sullivan, Jean-Pierre walked quickly through the shanty town which existed below the bluff of Natchez. It was readily apparent to a seasoned traveler of river towns that this section was no more than a pit of gambling and drinking. He knew it to be the kind of place where a traveler could be separated quickly from his money, and possibly even his life.

At the end of what served as a street, he saw a tent and frame dwelling set against the steep bluff. A wooden sign in the shape of a nose, dyed a deep blue with indigo hung above the door. The front was littered with broken casks, boxes, bottles and drunken river men, all lying about like so much waste. As Jean-Pierre approached, he could begin to hear the sounds of the Blue Nose as opposed to those of the other places nearby. There was a different tone which caught Jean-Pierre's ear immediately, something not of merriment but of anger. Stepping quickly now, he pushed aside the canvas flap with his left hand while placing his right upon the butt of one of the new pistols.

Upon entering, he took in at a glance what was happening. The many customers had separated off to the sides, leaving two men squared off in the middle of the dirt floor. One was Monsieur MacDuff and the other was a younger man who was dressed as a gambler. From appearances, they had been fighting for several minutes, as their clothes were torn and blood ran from each in several places. Around them, the floor was littered with cards, coins, cups, and the slosh of spilled liquor.

Monsieur MacDuff showed himself to be an aggressive fighter, true to his Scottish heritage. But the gambler was a much younger man. He was also taller and well versed in rough-and-tumble fighting. Again and again, they exchanged heavy blows, each somehow holding their footing. At one point the gambler grabbed the Patroon's shaggy hair and jerked his head forward, wrapping an arm around it in a locking hold. As if the hold were not enough the gambler then bit down on his adversary's right ear and pulled savagely. Bellowing out in pain, the Patroon reached back and found one of the gambler's eyes with his thumb. As he pushed in and twisted, the eye almost popped out before the gambler let go of the ear and hid his eyes behind the keelboatman's head. Thus pinned against the gambler, Monsieur MacDuff was choking for air and reaching vainly for something to grab.

Keelboatmen were known as rough fighters, and Monsieur MacDuff proved to be no less. His years on the river had taught him some tricks of his own. Bracing himself with his left foot, he used his right leg to lift the right leg of the gambler. Then he shifted all his weight backward. With only one leg on the floor and all the heavy keelboatman's weight hanging on him, the young gambler fell heavily to the floor.

When they struck the floor, the gambler lost his grip. This was what Monsieur MacDuff had counted on. With all the speed his battered body could muster, he lifted himself to his feet and then dropped himself into the gambler's chest, with his knees making contact. There was a sound of rushing air, and the gambler went limp. Thereupon the Patroon proceeded to pound the face of his adversary with his fists.[92]

The Patroon stopped, and seeing no response from the gambler, got up, shakily trying to catch his breath. Jean-Pierre had been watching the crowd during the fight, looking for any friend of the gambler who might interfere in the fight. The keelboat crew had stood back, allowing their Patroon to fight his own battle.

A roguish-looking character standing near the bar caught Jean-Pierre's attention. His facial expressions and eyes betrayed an allegiance to the gambler and therefore a danger to Monsieur MacDuff. Now with the gambler beaten and the Patroon's broad back exposed to him, the rogue raised his right arm, with the hand holding a long knife. Surely his intent was to throw the long blade into MacDuff's back.

In an instant Jean-Pierre's right hand brought up a pistol, cocking the weapon in the same movement. Instinctively, he pointed and fired into the man. Smoke belched bluish-black and the roar of the exploding powder momentarily silenced the screams of the crowd. The knife thrower now stood in agony against an upturned cask. His right arm hung in a twisted fashion with blood running off the hand in a stream. Turning his gaze to the crew, Jean-Pierre in a steady and authoritative voice said, "Bring along your Patroon, quickly." All of them instantly moved upon his order, two of them supporting their injured Patroon out of the tavern. Jean-Pierre covered their retreat with the other pistol which had appeared in his left hand immediately after the shot. The crowd here in the Blue

---

92   Frontiersmen of this era fought a rough-and-tumble style, often with no more rules than no knives or guns. Eye-gouging and ear biting were common.

Nose was as cruel and mean as ever assembled anywhere, but not a man moved even a hand as Jean-Pierre backed his way through the canvas.

Once outside they hurried along with some of the more sober ones watching the rear. Upon reaching their keelboat a few minutes later, Jean-Pierre continued his command of the situation. "Put Monsieur MacDuff aboard and tend to his wounds," he called to the two carrying him. To the other, he called, "Some of you bring *The Lassie* alongside the *New Orleans*. The others follow me to ready our cargo. We must hurry."

Filled with the urgency of the moment, not a man questioned his right to command. Having worked together many times before, they knew what to do. Several went with Jean-Pierre to locate their cargo. The others untied the keelboat and quickly poled it alongside the *New Orleans* to speed the loading process. In less than an hour everything was transferred to *The Lassie*. A watch was kept for the crowd of the Blue Nose, but the shift of cargo went by without incident.

With no reason to remain in Natchez and many reasons to leave, Jean-Pierre called to the crew as he stepped from the *New Orleans*, "Now, upriver with all speed." As the crew scrambled to their positions, the boss took his place at the bow while eight men eagerly manned the oars. They poled far enough away from the *New Orleans* for the oars to be used. Slowly they moved away from the Natchez landing and upstream along the eastern bank. All the while their Patroon lay below on a pallet of blankets.

Just before nightfall, Jean-Pierre directed them into a channel between a willow-covered island and the main bank. Here they tied off to cook their supper and rest. At this point they had no fear of being followed by anyone from Natchez. The fiddler broke out his instrument and from his place above the fire on the sand bar, drew out plaintive tunes of Scotland. In this manner, they found solace from the events of the afternoon.

By morning Monsieur MacDuff had recovered enough to resume command. He repeatedly thanked Jean-Pierre for saving not only his life, but his cargo and crew. To the entire crew, Jean-Pierre represented a savior, larger than life. Each of them realized the value of his actions in the heat of a dangerous situation.

At their noon stop, the cook, a man named Underhill, was tending to Monsieur MacDuff's wounds. With what medicine they had he was trying to bring some relief. The cook's pain killer was raw whiskey, which the patient was drinking copiously. "Patroon, this her' ear of yourn's not goin' ta heal wi' out bein' a ragged thang. I better go on and cut this dangly piece off and be done wi' it," stated the cook.

Nodding his reluctant approval, MacDuff took another long draw from the whiskey jug before the cutting began. The Patroon of this rough lot of men sat quietly as a sharp knife cut away the small amount of flesh holding on the top of the ear.

"Boss, ya shore air lucky, enyhow," stated Underhill.

"Lucky! What do ya' mean, lucky? Thet card sharp bit off most of my ear, after he cheated me, not ta' mention the bruises and broken ribs I'm a sufferin' with. How in thunder do ya' figure I'm lucky?" asked the Patroon.

"Cuz, iffen he'd bit offen the whole ear, ya'd be a marked man. Folks would think ya'd taken advantage of a woman and had been marked fer life," explained Underhill.[93]

---

93   94 Men who sexually abused a woman had an ear cut off, possibly

"Wal, guess you're right 'bout thet," responded Monsieur MacDuff, "shore wouldn't want folks a thinkin' I was thet kind of a feller."

After a few thoughtful moments, Monsieur MacDuff said, "Jean-Pierre, I'm still amazed at your shootin'. Why they tell me thet ya busted thet feller's shoulder bone plumb through, an' on a quickie shot too. Surely, ya' didn't hev' any time to aim thet pistol. Why, I don't know of anybody up er' down this her' river thet could've done it. No sir."

"But, Monsieur," replied Jean-Pierre with a tinge of both humor and embarrassment, "I did not aim for his shoulder at all, but for his chest."

The entire crew roared in laughter at Jean-Pierre's admission. His straightforward confession of almost having missed the man entirely did not sway in the least their high regard for him as being a great man of the river. In the years to come these men would, again and again, relate the tale of the tavern fight and how it ended, complete with their own lengthy and colorful embellishments. The challenges of frontier life gave opportunities for men to rise to almost mythical figures when heroic feats were coupled with a zest for storytelling.

It was several weeks later when the keelboat rowed its way into the landing at Poste aux Arkansas. Monsieur LeFlore was waiting at the landing with great excitement. Apparently, one of his clerks had seen them coming and had signaled their arrival.

---

both, and were flogged. The missing ear marked them for life. But since saloon fighting often involved ear biting, a man might lose an ear in a fight. In this case, some courthouses would issue an affidavit stating that the bearer had committed no crime wherein the punishment had exacted an ear.

Calling out even before the keelboat reached the landing, Monsieur LeFlore asked with laughter, "Did you have a good trip, Jean-Pierre? I suppose you had much fun in Nouvelle Orleans and Natchez, Oui?"

"Oui, Monsieur, but maybe too much excitement for this Frenchman. I believe I prefer the land of the Arkansas as it is not so dangerous as places like Nouvelle Orleans and Natchez," replied Jean-Pierre.

"Well, you are here and safe, that is what matters. And have you brought the supplies I ordered?" asked Monsieur LeFlore.

"Oui, Monsieur, the supplies are all here, just as you requested," answered Jean-Pierre.

With the boat tied off, the post staff and the crew began unloading *The Lassie*. Jean-Pierre then withdrew the leather wallet Monsieur LeFlore gave him at the beginning of the voyage.

"Here, Monsieur, are the papers detailing the sale of your furs and other stores as well as the purchase of the supplies you see here," stated Jean-Pierre.

"Merci beaucoup, Oh, mon Dieu. I am so thankful to you, Jean-Pierre," joyfully replied Monsieur LeFlore as they embraced.

Everyone was happy to have the journey completed. That evening after all the new stores were stowed away, Monsieur LeFlore expressed his appreciation to Jean-Pierre and Monsieur MacDuff's crew by giving them a feast. They talked into the night, exchanging stories and well wishes from Nouvelle Orleans. Of course, the tales of the jail break and the tavern fight in Natchez were the high-lights, by this time embellished greatly. Monsieur LeFlore was all the more impressed with Jean-Pierre Villeneuve.

Early the next morning Jean-Pierre surprised everyone by

announcing that he would be leaving immediately to head up the Mississippi. Monsieur MacDuff and his crew, those who were not still drunk from the night before, wished him well and offered him space on their boat any time.

Just before his departure, Monsieur LeFlore called Jean-Pierre to the main counter in the post. He embraced and kissed him in the fashion of the French, again thanking him for his great service. To further express his appreciation, he extended a small leather poke of Spanish bits which he said Jean-Pierre might find of value sometime, though he knew that trappers and traders typically did not use money.[94] Also, he lifted up a brightly polished rifle, saying it was his way of hoping Jean-Pierre would again bring meat to his fire.

Jean-Pierre was overwhelmed at the generosity of the gifts, particularly the rifle. It was certainly more carefully crafted than any rifle he had ever owned. The long rifle was a .45 caliber with a full stock beautifully decorated in silver. From its style and beautiful craftsmanship he knew it probably came from Pennsylvania. His emotion and pride in being given such a gift caused him to resolve to keep it all his life.[95]

---

94 Our modern monetary term "bit," is derived from the Spanish practice of taking coins and chopping them with an axe into eight bits. This was done as there were so few coins in circulation for exchange.

95 The American muzzle-loading rifle largely got its origin among the German rifle makers in Pennsylvania. Their creation was accurate, reliable and aesthetically beautiful. Though common rifles were simply iron fitted, many others were fitted in brass and pewter. A gentleman's rifle might be decorated in silver. As the rifles of Pennsylvania and Virginia were carried westward, they became known as Kentucky rifles, though there really was no such item as a Kentucky rifle. It should be noted that hunters and local gunsmiths would develop a unique style common to that region and time.

Later, as Jean-Pierre paddled down the Riviere Arkansas, he thought back to the good friendships he had made and vowed to return.

Chapter Eight

Ste. Genevieve

Jean-Pierre dug his paddle deep into the waters of the Riviere Arkansas this bright summer morning. Going downstream on such a major river usually required only minimal effort with the paddle, just enough to keep the pirogue under full control. But on this trip, he was paddling hard. Like many men who lived on the frontier, he found great satisfaction and even joy in being able to push himself day after day to the limits of his ability. And of course, he had been away from Ste. Genevieve[96] far longer than planned when he last left. He knew that some of his friends might even have thought him lost to the great earthquake, as they knew he was to have been in the Grand Marais at the time. By now most people up and down the river knew that area had received the worst of the damage.

The hard physical exertion he used paddling with the current insured that he was making good time on his journey back to Ste. Genevieve. It also freed his mind to reflect on the events of his prolonged absence. The past months had been rewarding in both furs and friends. The trip to Nouvelle Orleans with the keelboat

---

96 97 Ste. Genevieve, the oldest French settlement in Missouri, was a farming village as opposed to St. Louis, which was a trading post. In their rivalry, St. Louis residents called Ste. Genevieve "la misere" (miserable place) for its propensity to flood. The residents of Ste. Genevieve called St. Louis "pain cort" (short of bread) because they did not raise enough wheat to feed themselves.

crew and the ride back up river upon the New Orleans had shown him things that many trappers would never see in their entire lives. The memory of missing the Lewis and Clark expedition did not seem so bad now, as he thought of his many adventures over the years. Reflecting on all these things made his paddling seem effort-less and he made good time with the flow of the current.

In the early afternoon, he reached the cut-off to the Riviere Blanche. Monsieur LeFlore had told him that the keelboat crews regularly used it to save many leagues of travel. He left the Arkansas and paddled his way toward the clearer waters of the Blanche once again. The channel was large in itself and allowed for easy travel. At dusk he put his pirogue to the channel bank. After making a quick camp some yards back from the edge of a steep bank, he returned to the water's edge and moved the pirogue to a more concealed loca-tion. From this point on he would have to be wary of river pirates. Being alone compounded the danger as those pirates mostly worked in large groups and preyed on small groups or lone travelers.

By daylight the next morning, Jean-Pierre was a league farther down the channel toward the Riviere Blanche. When he reached that waterway, he took the time to check on his raft. He no longer needed it, but still held some small affection for the craft. He found it was tied just as he had left it, hidden in a patch of briars. Jean-Pierre left it there, for he knew that in the wilderness a cache of any kind could in the future mean the difference between life and death.

About noon he reached the Fleuve Mississippi.[97] Turning upstream, he paddled a course that kept him an equal distance between the main current and the western bank. The main current

---

97   This location was later known as Montgomery Point for the owner of a trading post located there.

was too strong to paddle against easily, and the river bank offered places where pirates might hide for an ambush. Hour after hour, he paddled this course all day. Just before nightfall, he chose a camp on the inside edge of one of the river's many willow-covered islands. Always cautious, he took steps to hide his pirogue and douse his cook fire before darkness set in. He did not want to advertise his campsite to anyone else on this stretch of the river.

Day after day he continued upriver. By now his muscles were back in tone with the work of the paddle. He trailed a fishing line behind the boat and depended on the fish he caught to supplement his supply of dried meat.

Four days upstream from his entrance into the Mississippi, Jean-Pierre noticed a small river entering from the west. He believed that this must be the mouth of the St. Francois. This is where he would have entered the Mississippi if his plans had not been upset by the earthquake. Just as he had not gone with the Lewis and Clark party, he had not been able to follow the St. Francois. Jean-Pierre told himself that he could not live centered around what might have happened, but in what did happen. And, he reminded himself, this trip had been both eventful and rewarding.

Passing the St. Francois, Jean-Pierre continued upriver at his fast pace. The Mississippi was so large that it was possible for him to avoid the strong current. Of course, he had to work around the shifting currents of the many bends in the channel. He was glad he had sold his furs at Poste aux Arkansas as the absence of heavy cargo made his work much lighter. And, William Talbot's handi-work paid off here; the pirogue was well trimmed and required only a minimum of effort to move it forward.

Without event, other than the frequently passing flatboat or keelboat, he arrived at Hopefield.[98] Benjamin Fooy himself met Jean-Pierre at the landing. Having known Jean-Pierre almost all his life, Fooy immediately invited him to refreshments. Fooy's servants set out cold sliced bear meat, bread, butter, fried fish, and, knowing the ways of the French, hot coffee. The two men sat and shared news for several hours. Fooy was quite interested in affairs from the southern portion of the Mississippi and the Arkansas. He said that he had known Monsieur LeFlore at Poste aux Arkansas when he had acted as Indian Agent to the Chickasaw at Fort Barrancas de Margos.

Jean-Pierre's inquiry about the French settlements farther upriver brought much the same reports he had heard before. Fooy did add that Little Prairie had been totally deserted due to the fear caused by the earthquake.[99] On a positive note, he reported

---

98   In 1795, the United States effected a new treaty with Spain, the Treaty of San Lorenzo. Under this treaty, Spain withdrew its border southward from Tennessee to the 31st parallel. Spain's Fort Barrancas de Margos, at the present site of Memphis, Tennessee, had to be abandoned. Its small military detachment simply crossed the Mississippi River into Arkansas and built a new fort, Campo del Esperanza. The Spanish Indian agent, Benjamin Fooy, moved with them and established his own settlement near the fort. Campo del Esperanza translates from Spanish to English as field of hope, so Fooy's settlement came to be known as Hopefield. A marker locates the site as just north of Interstate 40 near the bank of the Mississippi River. It, along with several other southern river towns, was burned by Northern gunboats during the Civil War. During the 1920's, a flood washed away all that remained. It was never rebuilt, though West Memphis, Arkansas is located nearby.
The reader might need to be reminded that the Louisiana Purchase did not occur until 1803 and that the Louisiana region was under Spanish control until the Americans took possession in 1804.

99   Some towns became deserted because the fear experienced by the people was too great. It is no wonder after three major earthquakes and 1800 tremors over four months. Little Prairie, now Caruthersville, Missouri, was such a town.

that from the almost daily tremors since December, most people were getting used to the earth shaking and some communities had regained their normal routine.

Because Fooy had acted as Indian agent to the Chickasaw, Jean-Pierre particularly asked him about his mother's people and certain members with whom he might still have contact. Fooy replied that since he was only across the river from the main Chickasaw territory, he traded with them regularly and kept up with the activities of the tribe.[100] By now they were adopting many white man's ways; planting more crops, building cabins, and wearing linsey-woolsey, as well as owning black slaves and drinking whiskey. Some of them were also getting an education and embracing Christianity.

Located in the middle Mississippi Valley, Fooy was able to watch the changes among the tribes due to the white man's expansion. Some Delaware and Shawnee had been living west of the Mississippi since 1790. The Spanish accepted them as a buffer between the white settlers along the Mississippi and the ever hostile Osage to the west. This relocation had angered the Osage, giving them less area to move about. And the Cherokee had been granted a very large area north of the Riviere Arkansas and to the east of the mountains. This upset not only the Osage but also the Quapaw who resided along the lower Arkansas. He also told of the eastern tribes, the Cherokee and Creek, selling land to the whites which they did

---

100   The Chickasaw people were later designated by the U.S. Congress to be one of the five civilized tribes (Muskogee, or Creek, Seminole, Cherokee, Choctaw, and Chickasaw). Their primary home area at this time was northern Mississippi, northwestern Alabama, and western Tennessee. They were a small tribe in comparison to the Choctaw but ranged from the Ohio to the Gulf and from Alabama to the Arkansas River. They were the only tribe never subjugated by the French or Spanish, choosing to place their loyalty with the British. Some scholars believe that it was the Chickasaw who almost destroyed the De Soto expedition.

not even claim but was really that of another tribe.[101] White speculators were rushing ahead of the settlers to secure whatever land could be bought and resold at a tremendous profit.

Fooy talked of the transition between French and Spanish and American and Indian. He told how when the Spanish were forced to abandon Fort Barrancas de Margos by the Americans in 1797, he had crossed the river with them to this location. With no Indians to serve as agent, he had built a trading post and stayed when the Spanish later moved on downriver.

River traffic had dramatically increased. Now keelboats and flatboats plied the Mississippi on a daily basis, hauling great loads of freight. Of course, there was now talk of a steamboat that could come up the Mississippi against the current even as far as the Ohio and possibly to St. Louis.[102] Jean-Pierre interjected a short account of his ride aboard the New Orleans upriver to Natchez. Fooy speculated that it was only a matter of time before he watched steamboats out on the river just as now he watches the keelboats and flatboats.

Jean-Pierre had heard bits and pieces of these things but had never heard them put together as Fooy had on this afternoon. Truly, he had seen many changes over the years of his life and yet it seemed

---

101 The Great Bend area was sold more than once to greedy Americans by tribes who did not in truth possess it. This region was bounded by the curving Tennessee River on the south and the state of Tennessee on the North. During this time period, that great curve of the Tennessee River from southward, to westward, and back to northward was called the Great Bend. This term "great bend" was given to other river areas, such as the Arkansas in the state of Kansas and the Red where it connects with the state of Arkansas.

102 The first steamboat reached St. Louis in 1817. But its efforts were so weak that it had to be poled at times like a keelboat. It took some years of engineering improvements to develop a steamboat powerful enough to ascend the major rivers.

that the greater changes were yet to come.

At the end of their conversation, a man sitting at another table surprised Jean-Pierre when he spoke. Jean-Pierre had seen him in the room but had given him little notice. Addressing himself to Jean-Pierre in a hesitant manner, he said, "Monsieur Villeneuve, allow me to introduce myself. My name is Henry Blackwater, of London. I heard you were going upriver in your canoe. Might I get a ride with you to St. Louis, if you are going that far."

Glancing briefly toward Benjamin Fooy for a clue as to the character of this man, Jean-Pierre replied, "Monsieur, I do have the space in my pirogue, but I am traveling long days, working very hard at the paddle. Can you paddle a pirogue?"

"Well, yes sir, I can, and I'd be a help to you as well, with the two of us, we'd go even faster," answered the Englishman eagerly.

Benjamin Fooy looked at Jean-Pierre as if to say, the choice is yours, saying only, "Mister Blackwater is an English scholar over here studying us frontier types. He caught a ride down from Cincinnati on a keelboat, but wants to get back up to St. Louis. Seems like a nice fellow, even if he is English."[103]

At this last statement, the Englishman nodded his head in agreement. Perplexed at the odd situation, Jean-Pierre paused and thought. He did not want the responsibility of someone who could not take care of himself and might slow him down. But it was his nature to be hospitable to others. "Very well, Monsieur, if it pleases you. We shall leave just before the light," relented Jean-Pierre.

---

103   Several English writers as well as one German traveled through the region of the Arkansas from 1818 to 1840 (Nuttall, Schoolcraft, Flint, Gerstacker) and kept daily journals which were later published upon their return. They commented in some detail on the plant and animal life, terrain, travel conditions, and the existing population.

Surprisingly, Henry Blackwater was ready and sitting in front of Benjamin Fooy's fireplace the next morning when Jean-Pierre left his sleeping quarters. With no more than a cup of coffee and a good-bye to the Fooy household, Jean-Pierre led his new companion through the dim morning light to the landing and shoved off in the pirogue.

It did not take the trapper long to realize that the Englishman knew little about paddles and pirogues. However, he was an eager student and followed directions well. By the end of their first day together, Henry Blackwater made up for the extra weight he added to the craft.

Every night Jean-Pierre took extra precautions, as this was a stretch of river well known for river pirates. These were largely American criminals who had moved westward to avoid capture. Here, they worked their treachery in a region where there was little chance of getting caught. Often working in large groups, they preyed upon isolated travelers, either flatboats on the rivers or foot travelers on the Natchez Trace. Because of the severe penalty imposed for piracy, they rarely left witnesses. Each evening, Jean-Pierre selected a hidden camp before dark and finished their cook-fire before the flames could be seen at any distance. Some nights he purposely moved their camp some distance upriver after dusk to hide the location of their night camp. This way he hoped to protect himself and Monsieur Blackwater during the night.

Several days passed without incident. But the time came when their luck ran out. Jean-Pierre had them in the slower current on the west side of the river when he noticed a camp on a point to their left. A cook-fire was burning, and a pirogue was tied up to some driftwood at the river's edge. As they passed by, Jean-Pierre did not like the stare of the four men at the fire. At first, Jean-Pierre said nothing to the Englishman as these men might be only travelers like themselves.

To be on the safe side, after they passed to the left around the point and out of sight of the camp, he told Monsieur Blackwater to increase his pace. When they were no more than a third of the way to the next bend, a glance over his shoulder revealed that the men from the camp were now coming upriver in their pirogue. Again, Jean-Pierre told himself that these could be just travelers. The fact that they were gaining was probably due to there being several men in the craft to paddle. Also, these men would be fresher after resting. Monsieur Blackwater added little to their own speed.

Jean-Pierre was greatly troubled by a plume of dark smoke that was now rising from the men's camp on the point. Before, it had barely put off any smoke. The dry driftwood, long piled up on the point by past flooding, would make a smokeless fire. But a pile of green willow limbs would put off such smoke. He also knew that such smoke could be seen from a great distance upriver.

Jean-Pierre began to look at their options. Assuming that these were river pirates, he knew that the two of them could land opposite the Chickasaw Bluffs which they were approaching and make a stand or flee into the timber and hide. The bluffs themselves would not afford protection as their steepness would make flight from the river difficult.[104] But a standing fight against four armed men might not turn out well, particularly since they could land at another location and approach them from four different directions.

---

104 Chickasaw Bluffs were the high earthen bluffs which rise from the Mississippi River in western Tennessee. The fourth is at the present site of Memphis. The first, second, and third are located upriver, each separated from the others by only a few miles.

Or, the pirates could steal their pirogue, leaving them afoot. Neither of these options appealed to Jean-Pierre.

Jean-Pierre gave some thought to turning back downriver to the Fourth Chickasaw Bluff, as protection would be afforded by the American garrison at Fort Pickering. But it was too far away, and besides, the supposed threat was now between them and the fort.

They could also try for their best speed and attempt to outrun the pirates, at least until a place of safety was sighted. Certainly, a keelboat or a flatboat would be very welcome now. But as the other pirogue was gaining already, he was skeptical that their best effort could out pace the pirates for any length of time. Also, the farther they went upriver, the closer they might be getting to whomever the smoke signal was intended for.

Again, the thought came to Jean-Pierre that these might only be common travelers and of no danger. But the risk was too great for him to accept that assumption at this point. In a desperate move, Jean-Pierre took the option with which he was most comfortable at this time. Calling to Monsieur Blackwater, he said, "Monsieur, we're going to hold to the middle of the river now. We need all your strength at the paddle. The channel will be difficult due to the current. And this channel will have many snags."

"Yes, of course, but isn't there an easier route? We've never gone against the channel current before," asked the Englishman, as he dug in the paddle faster and deeper.

"I must tell you, Monsieur, there is another pirogue behind us which I fear contains the river pirates. And they are gaining upon us now. If we take the harder channel, that will give them the opportunity of passing around the easier channel to the left, or the shorter channel to the right. We will stop and rest at the head of the island.

If they pass on by, then my fear was for nothing. At least, by giving them a choice of the easier or the shorter channels, we will learn for certain who they are.

Jean-Pierre was familiar with this stretch of the river. He knew that the third, second and first of the Chickasaw Bluffs ran along the river's east bank for the next several miles. There were many hiding places for pirates among the islands and backwater channels. The bend itself was called the Devil's Elbow for its sharpness.

Looking over his left shoulder at the other pirogue, Monsieur Blackwater made efforts that Jean-Pierre did not know he had. Together they braved the strong current of the middle channel. To their dismay, scarcely had they made their turn when the other craft did the same, confirming Jean-Pierre's fears. Stroke after furious stroke, the race was on now, and against the current of the mighty river. Not only was it a race of speed, but the numerous snags required great skill to avoid upsetting their pirogue. But, the channel was difficult also for their pursuers. As they worked through the upper end of the chute, Jean-Pierre was sure that they had actually widened the gap between them. His skill at guiding the pirogue may have made the difference. Now a plan was forming in Jean-Pierre's mind to attempt another test. He thought that if they swung left across the river, they could find refuge in the large willow island which he knew to run along that side of the river. And, just possibly, the men following might continue on upriver. Certainly, both he and Monsieur Blackwater would enjoy a rest.

By the time they neared the head of the island, both men were almost spent, but they pushed on due to the danger of the situation. It was some relief to them that the pirates had slowed somewhat through the chute. Pushing against the current around the head of the island, Jean-Pierre saw relief in a chain of willow-covered islands along the right bank. There was every possibility that they could hide themselves there.

It was Monsieur Blackwater who dashed Jean-Pierre's hopes with his cry and gesture upriver to the right bank. There, setting out, was a skiff[105] with several men aboard. It was heading downstream with the current. Neither had to say that if the skiff continued, it would intercept their own course.

With fear in his voice, Monsieur Blackwater called back, "are those men pirates as well, Monsieur Villeneuve?"

"Oui, Monsieur, I believe so," answered Jean-Pierre.

After a pause of dismay, Jean-Pierre called forward, "To the right, Monsieur Blackwater, we will attempt to find some refuge along the eastern bank. Paddling now with all their remaining strength, the two travelers pushed directly across the main current. It was useless now to attempt to hide themselves immediately as the men in the skiff had already seen them. Now Jean-Pierre pushed on in an attempt to somehow find concealment in one of the backwaters along that side of the river. Apparently, those in the pirogue to the rear realized this area presented an opportunity for their prey to escape, for they now began firing. Though none of their shots came very close, they did nothing to calm the fears of the travelers. Directing the pirogue into a channel which opened before them, Jean-Pierre kept the men behind them from having a clear shot. Hopefully, this would buy Jean-Pierre some time to gain a suitable refuge.

---

105   The English skiff was a small craft constructed of planks. It had a flat bottom which tapered up in the front and straight up sides. The author believes that it may be the forerunner of today's Southern John boat.

This channel was well hidden from the main river so the men in the skiff could not see them. Jean-Pierre's sharp eye had noted four men in the skiff, with three at the oars. The fourth had stood in the front, probably the leader of the entire group.

He called to the Englishman to slow his pace, as their danger had lessened for the time being and their strength would need to be conserved for later. He knew that the pirates in the pirogue would be following, but they were likely as tired as Jean-Pierre and Monsieur Blackwater. For now, they would press on while looking for a refuge. The muddy banks would not allow them to get out of the pirogue without leaving tracks to alert their pursuers. Besides, to make a stand and fight was the last resort as Monsieur Blackwater was not his responsibility and Jean-Pierre did not believe the Englishman could keep himself from being captured if they were separated. So, for now, they kept on steadily in hope.

For more than an hour, they kept on up this backwater channel. Though they saw nothing of the pirogue behind them, they were certain that it was following. Jean-Pierre knew that this one channel was fed by three outlets from the main river. Through one of these they must pass to regain the Mississippi. He was certain that the river pirates were also familiar with the channels. In all likelihood, the pirates in the skiff would come down through one of those outlets.

After some time they came onto the first channel, but Jean-Pierre pushed them on by as he feared the skiff would more likely be coming that way. In hushed tones, he called upon Monsieur Blackwater to paddle with all his speed now. Jean-Pierre was impressed with the Englishman's determination as he was surely almost exhausted from the continued racing upstream.

Soon after they passed the next bend, they both heard loud voices behind them. As these voices became less distinct, they determined that the pirates in the skiff had passed from the first outlet channel into the single channel going downstream. Knowing that it would only be a short time before the skiff met the pirogue and both hurried upstream after them, Jean-Pierre and Monsieur Blackwater labored with what little speed their tired arms could produce.

The Frenchman passed by the next outlet channel and continued on toward the last, which left the river near the Third Chickasaw Bluff. At the upper end of the third outlet channel, the main river opened before them. It was tempting to set out across the wide channel of almost one-third of a league. But Jean-Pierre knew that their pursuers were only a short distance behind them and would very soon come to the main channel themselves. He also knew that he and Monsieur Blackwater were too exhausted to outdistance the pirates on the open river. There the pirates in two crafts could easily separate and come at their quarry from two sides. Some would be able to shoot rifles while others rowed or paddled. Jean-Pierre saw the open river now as a hopeless situation.

Remembering a myriad of islands a short way back down the channel, he turned their pirogue back in that direction. These were all heavily covered in willows and would offer places for them to hide. Monsieur Blackwater looked dumbfounded and turned as if to ask what they were doing in going back in the direction of their enemies.

"To find a cache for ourselves, Monsieur, for on the open river I am afraid we would be quickly caught," explained the Frenchman.

With great cheer, Jean-Pierre called for Monsieur Blackwater to paddle the harder as these islands could afford them safety.[106] Into the channels among the small islands the pirogue shot, sending the draping branches streaming. Through and around, Jean-Pierre used all his skills from a lifetime of river travel to ply a course deeper into this refuge without damaging any vegetation or soil which would give away their direction of travel. Several cranes flew away in their wake, and Jean-Pierre hoped that their pursuers were too far away to notice.

As they began to near the edge of the third bluff, Jean-Pierre began to look for where they might possibly hide, but if not, then fort up and fight it out with the pirates. As they were near the bluff, abandoning the pirogue to flee on foot was now another option for them. Sighting what looked to have potential, he eased the pirogue behind a screening of bushes. Leaving the craft hidden, the two desperate travelers dashed into the willow thicket with all their weapons. Here Jean-Pierre directed Monsieur Blackwater to a hollow in the sand created by a swirl during high water. The hollow was about two feet deep and ten feet across. It was open at one end where the sand had been washed out. This opening was closed off with a fallen tree and much dead brush, providing a visual barrier to anyone from that side. The two sat there taking long breaths and letting their muscles relax after the strenuous effort to outrun the pirates.

Here, Jean-Pierre arranged his weapons; the Pennsylvania rifle, the French musket, the brace of pistols and his ash bow. Of

---

106 The channels, islands, currents and terrain features referred to during this scene existed as they are portrayed. The 1814 edition of the "Navigator," published two years after this fictional situation, maps the river features as presented in the story.

course, he always carried a long knife and tomahawk. In close quarters, these weapons had proven in times past to be very effective. Monsieur Blackwater had only an English fowling piece which he held in shaking hands.[107] Truly, this experience had already unnerved him. But, without doubt it would get worse in the next few minutes as soon as one of the pirate craft found them. As the cluster of islands was small, it was only a matter of time.

Out of concern for Monsieur Blackwater's ability to remain silent, Jean-Pierre softly said, "Now, Monsieur, it is most important that we make no sounds to give away our position. There are many of the pirates, so we must have every advantage."

The Englishman turned and nodded a blanched face toward Jean-Pierre. "Let us hope and pray, Monsieur, that the pirates do not find us at all and go away," added Jean-Pierre to calm his traveling companion. He himself did not believe that there was any chance of this.

For several long moments, they crouched there in the sand with sweat dripping off their bodies. Mosquitoes swarmed around them and out in the channel, a water moccasin swam across to the far side of the channel to disappear in the undergrowth.

Mentally, Jean-Pierre went over in his mind how the attack might proceed. It was his expectation that the two crafts would separate so that both channels could be checked at once. And, upon not seeing them on the open river, they would likely check back along the outlets where the two may have hidden. He thought that the pirates would continue on in their water craft as that would

___

107   An English fowling piece was an early shotgun, designed to shoot shot at waterfowl and upland birds. Their barrels had thin walls, but their stock and firing mechanism resembled the rifles of the day.

be quieter than walking. Hopefully, only one craft would come at a time. And, hopefully, they would give up the search and return across the river. Jean-Pierre did not hold out for the latter.

Here they could make a good fight of it with the sand bar to protect and conceal them. They had brought food and water from the pirogue as well as all their weapons, powder, and shot. Unfortunately, Jean-Pierre deemed the Englishman's fowling piece about as worthless as the Englishman himself in a fight such as the one before them.

Then he heard an approaching craft and looked left to see the skiff come into view. In just a moment or two it would pass by the pirogue. Jean-Pierre and Monsieur Blackwater would be fortunate if the pirates did not see the pirogue in the weeds. Peering through the thick willow branches, Jean-Pierre could see that the man in the front was standing with his rifle upraised at the ready. The middle two men were slowly working the oars while the man in the rear kept watch with his rifle across his lap.

Rapidly, Jean-Pierre thought of what might be necessary to turn the situation around. It occurred to him that a Chickasaw war party would be a welcome sight right now. Though this was Chickasaw territory, he had not seen any of his kinsmen during the entire trip up the river. The thought came to him that these pirates might not know that there were no Chickasaws about the river. Then he knew what he had to try if the pirates located the pirogue. For then a fight would be inevitable. Carefully laying aside the long rifle, Jean-Pierre picked up the bow and readied an arrow, all without taking his eyes off the pirates. Monsieur Blackwater watched this switch in disbelief and fear. But the Englishman sat silently and waited, as he still had some self-control.

It was then that the standing pirate called out that he had seen the pirogue, pointing it out with his rifle. The arrow slipped through the brush and into the man's chest so fast that no one in the skiff knew from where it came. Standing only briefly in shock, the pirate spasmed, causing him to lose his grip on his rifle. Then he dropped the rifle into the channel and fell back across the front oarsman, blood bubbling from his mouth.

Almost before he fell, another arrow found the man in the rear of the skiff. It was this man's good fortune that he turned at the same instant, resulting in the metal arrowhead only slicing a deep wound across the front of his chest. But he cried in pain as if he had been hurt badly. Now the oarsmen in the skiff began to panic, with a man on either side of them injured, and they still did not yet know from where the attack was coming. The arrows had further confused them as they had not anticipated any Indian involvement. Jean-Pierre knew that the Chickasaws more often fought with guns, but he had chosen to use the bow instead to help reinforce his illusion. Besides, his guns were ready if his illusion failed. But it had worked. In the minds of the pirates, they were now being attacked by a Chickasaw war party.

Playing upon their new-found fear, Jean-Pierre drew from within himself a quivering cry, rising and lowering, changing in pitch and volume. As he followed this cry with others equally as harrowing, he rained arrows upon the fleeing skiff. The pirates were now in a full panic, certain that they had stumbled into a Chickasaw war party. With great speed, the two oarsmen drove their scull out from the willow islands. There they met their confederates in the pirogue. After telling them of having been attacked by Indians, both crafts turned to cross the river with all speed. All of this was observed by Jean-Pierre who had climbed to the top of a large willow for an observation post.

A broad smile crossed his face as he dropped to the sand. "Monsieur, we sent them on the run. I think they want nothing more to do with this Chickasaw Indian," declared Jean-Pierre. Realizing now for the first time his companion's facial resemblance to the Indians, Henry Blackwater sat back and sighed deeply, wiping his brow with a monogrammed handkerchief.

After lifting Monsieur Blackwater to his feet, Jean-Pierre gathered his weapons and led the way back to the pirogue. Once aboard, he pushed the craft back out into the small channel and positioned them right above where the pirates' skiff had been during the brief skirmish. Reaching down to the bottom of the shallow channel, he felt about until he located the dropped rifle. After rinsing it of mud in the surface water, he shook it somewhat dry and laid it into the bottom of his pirogue. Also, he took the time to retrieve some of his arrows which were in sight.

Monsieur Blackwater was terrified to leave the sanctuary of the willow islands, but Jean-Pierre explained to him that they needed to be near the open channel in case the river pirates returned. He went on to say that once darkness settled, they would proceed upriver in safety.

One week later Jean-Pierre and Monsieur Blackwater passed New Madrid, giving Jean-Pierre his first look at this settlement since the earthquake. Though he had never lived here, he was familiar with the settlement and could see clearly that it indeed had sunk in elevation. The area of exposed soil nearby would have been the cemetery which had been thrown into the river. At the thought of dead people being tossed into the river, Jean-Pierre became quite uneasy and quickly crossed himself.

Of course, this was not the first effects of the quake they had observed on their trip upriver. In many places, the old faces of the river bluffs had fallen away under the stress of the shocks as the soft soil had given way. The land was still littered with driftwood and fallen trees from the woods along the river.

A few days later they passed Cape Girardeau[108] and a week after that they arrived at his beloved Ste. Genevieve. Stepping upon the bank, Jean-Pierre experienced something of wonder that he was indeed back after all his experiences since leaving last fall.

With Monsieur Blackwater in tow, it only required a little time to locate his friend, Louis Charlivoix, who was at leisure at his home. "Is that really you, mon ami? I was sure that the earth had opened up and swallowed you whole," cried the man with tears in his eyes.

The two good friends embraced and kissed as is the way of the French before standing back beaming to look at one another and laugh. "You thought I was swallowed up. Why, I thought this whole village might have been swallowed up, such was the rumbling of the earth," stated Jean-Pierre in relief in seeing that not only his old friend but his beloved town was safe. Taking time now to introduce Monsieur Blackwater and explain his desire to continue on to St. Louis, Jean-Pierre questioned Louis regarding any boat going there in the next few days. His friend informed them both that a large bateau was due to leave in two days and that he would secure the Englishman a space aboard it.

---

108   Cape Girardeau was settled in 1795. The Spanish used the area for the relocation of the Shawnee and Delawares. This town early on became mostly occupied by Americans. The author's family settled in the area in 1806 and were coopers by trade.

"But what happened to you after the great quake, Jean-Pierre?" asked Louis. "We were so worried about you when you did not return straightaway."

Shaking his head before answering, Jean-Pierre explained, "After the first quake, I had to walk west to safety. But without my fusil or my horse, as they were lost. From there I decided to complete my winter's trapping west of the great ridge, so I walked on as far as the Riviere Noire. From there I floated down to the Riviere Blanche and on that riviere to the Riviere Arkansas and Poste aux Arkansas. I even made a trip to Nouvelle Orleans on a keelboat and rode the new steamboat with the giant paddle which turns in the water. And, now I am here, again with my friend."

"But, Monsieur Villeneuve, you did not mention the river pirates who tried to kill us," added Monsieur Blackwater.

"Mon Dieu, but what experiences you have had. Earthquakes, keelboats, Nouvelle Orleans, steamboats, and river pirates. Now you will never run out of stories. And, what about this land of the Arkansas, how was it," asked Louis?

"Magnificent, so much so that I must return. There are many rivers to explore and trap and many possibilities for an old French trapper such as myself," declared Jean-Pierre.

"And leave me here," retorted Louis.

"Ah, you know that your good wife and children have a hold upon you far stronger than your desire to explore the rivers and trails," answered Jean-Pierre.

"Oui, that is true. Would that be why you never took a wife then, mon ami?" asked Louis.

"Part of it," replied Jean-Pierre reflectively. Henry Blackwater sat quietly and observed this conversation between these old friends.

By this time he was quite enamored with Jean-Pierre Villeneuve.

"At any rate, you will return to the land of the Arkansas and possibly die there, I can see it in your eyes, mon ami," stated Louis.

"A man must live and die somewhere," replied Jean-Pierre, "and this land of the Arkansas is an exciting place to do both, particularly in the years ahead."

Credits

Credit must be given for research materials to the following university libraries, listed in order of material used.

- Eastern Washington University
- Washington State University
- University of Oklahoma
- University of Memphis
- Arkansas Tech University
- Arkansas State University

Special recognition is given the following persons for their technical expertise, their editorial opinion, and their encouragement.

- Dr. William McNeil, Folklorist, Ozark Folk Center
- Dr. Leslie "Skip" Stewart-Abernathy, Survey Archaeologist, Arkansas Tech University
- Dr. Thomas DeBlack, Professor of History, Arkansas Tech University
- Morris Arnold, Historian of Colonial Arkansas
- Larry Willis, Arkansas History Teacher, Marmaduke High School
- Patricia Riviere-Mitchell, Native French
- Chaplain William Burke, Societe de Jesus
- Glenda Galvan, Curator, Chickasaw Nation Museum
- Ken Smith, Outdoorsman
- Chuck New, Outdoorsman

Great thanks is to be given to the author's many fans who have persisted in their demands for this novel to be published.

Special appreciation is to be expressed to Morris Arnold for the final edit and the writing of the preface.

No amount of credit given would be sufficient without that due the author's friend and fellow professional speaker Joe McBride. Joe not only edited and formatted this manuscript but edited and formatted the author's former historical novel, *Little Man,* as well. Without his effort and support, neither would likely have been published and available for readers.